NEWS AND NOODLES

A SMALL TOWN COZY MYSTERY

CARLY WINTER

Cover by
COVEREDBYMELINDA.COM
Edited by
DIVAS AT WORK EDITING

WESTWARD PUBLISHING / CARLY FALL, LLC

What happens when an alligator crashes a wedding?

Tilly's special day is ruined when not only does an alligator make an appearance, but the sound system goes down, it rains, the caterer delivers the wrong meal… and is later found dead.

Some of Tilly's family were the last ones to see the woman alive, and law enforcement believes one of them may be the murderer.

As Tilly rifles through the clues to find the real killer, she comes to believe someone sabotaged her wedding on purpose. But are the killer and saboteur the same dangerous person, or does she have two mysteries to solve?

CHAPTER 1

So much for my wedding being a non-stressful event.

"What do you mean my wedding dress is lost?" I screeched into the phone. "I'm supposed to get married *tomorrow* and the ticketing agent and the airport said you'd find it!"

"I'm sorry, ma'am," the agent drawled, his voice indicating he wasn't sorry at all. In fact, he sounded quite bored with the conversation. "We've tried to trace it, but the best we can tell it's either in Kansas City or Toronto. Maybe New Mexico."

"Canada? Toronto, Canada?!"

"Yes."

How could this be happening to me?

"You've lost my wedding dress! I'm getting married tomorrow! How am I supposed to get married without a dress?!"

"Once again, I apologize," he replied with a sigh. "I'll keep looking for it."

With a curse, I hung up the phone and tossed it on the couch. Mama came into the living room and sat down next to me.

"It's okay, Tilly," she said. "We'll go find another one."

"Their stupid slogan is, *we care about you*. They don't care about anything. The guy I just talked to made that quite obvious."

Angry tears welled in my eyes and tracked down my cheeks. I'd spent three months determined to fit into the dress, and I'd done it by cutting out all carbohydrates except leafy greens. I hadn't even touched any sugar-free treats. The dress had been perfect for me, and I had looked forward to wearing it on the day I would marry Derek.

"And it's not okay, Mama," I said through gritted teeth. "Those idiots at the airline can't find my dress! My *wedding* dress!"

"Honey, we'll get it worked out," she said, patting my hand. "Remember, the day isn't about a dress. It's about you and Derek and your feelings for each other."

I nodded, trying to understand her point of view. Of course, she was right, but I had wanted to wear *that* dress. Turning into a bridezilla the day before my wedding wasn't my intention, but I was darn close to growing claws and ripping down buildings.

"The caterer will be here soon to go over the last-minute details and setup," Mama said. "Why don't you head upstairs and get dressed?"

I glanced down at my pajamas. Derek and I had arrived in Louisiana the prior evening, and I hadn't slept well because of the time change. I'd been up since before dawn and hadn't dressed yet.

"Go on, honey. You don't want to meet Francois for the first time in your jammies. He owns Francois' Fancy Food Catering and is a highly respected member of our community."

I stood and headed up the stairs to the room where I'd spent my teenage years. Mama hadn't changed the furniture except she'd shoved the two twin beds into one and hung a baby blue comforter over them. It felt weird being home again, but I was glad Derek and I had agreed to marry at my parents' place. It would be a proverbial new start for me and I'd put my past behind me for good.

After pulling on a pair of jeans and a T-shirt, I glanced at my reflection in the mirror. The humidity hadn't done my hair any favors and I had no idea what to do with it for the wedding. Did I try to work with the frizz, or should I attempt to straighten it? Wear it in an updo?

"Figure that out later," I mumbled as I applied a little mascara.

The doorbell rang, and I hurried downstairs. Mama had hired Francois, and I had yet to meet the man in whom I'd entrusted my wedding day.

"Francois!" Mama greeted him. "Come in! Come in!"

Ah, love," he replied. "It's so wonderful to see you, Jennifer." I rounded the corner as he kissed her cheeks. It was weird hearing my mom referred to by her given name. Hank always called her a term of endearment, and she was always Mama to me.

"Is this the bride?" Francois asked as he brushed past my mom and over to me.

"Yes. That's my daughter, Tilly," Mama said.

"It's lovely to meet you," Francois crooned, his voice lilting with just a hint of a French accent. "You're going to be a stunning bride."

"The airline lost my dress, so I don't know about stunning," I said as I shook his hand. He stood a couple inches taller than me, thin as a rail with a notebook tucked under his arm, and I wondered if that skinny mustache was actually real, or if he'd pasted it on. Frankly, it seemed to sit a little off-center.

"*Mon Dieu!*" he exclaimed, his eyes like saucers. "What a horrible atrocity!"

"We're going shopping to replace it in a bit," Mama said. "The day isn't about the dress."

"You're so right, Jennifer," Francois replied. "It's about gathering to celebrate two people who are in love." He glanced around the foyer before leaning in, a mischievous grin on his face. "I once had to cater a nudist wedding. Trust me, no matter what happens tomorrow, no matter what you wear, it will never be as horrible as those four hours. I was permanently scarred. I'm surprised I'm not blind!"

Mama and I glanced at each other and burst out laughing, and my soul suddenly lightened. He was right. Everything would be okay, fancy wedding dress or not.

"Shall we go over the final menu?" Francois asked, hooking his arm through my mom's while leading us into the kitchen. "It's going to be a glorious day!"

We sat at the kitchen table and I gazed out the

floor to ceiling windows. The manicured grass littered with old, native oak and maple trees stretched about an acre to the water's edge while puffy white clouds hung above. A small deck with a covered trellis sat to the left of the door. Our ceremony would take place in the grassy area closest to the house. To the right of the house lay another clearing where Francois and his crew would set up our yummy buffet.

The company we'd rented the tables and chairs from had come yesterday before Derek and I arrived to set up everything, including the sound system. We weren't having a big wedding, but it was going to be very nice. Casually elegant, Mama had called it.

"Now, we agreed that a proper Creole menu would be appropriate," Francois said, opening his notebook. "What's a Louisiana wedding without all the good stuff?"

My mouth watered just thinking about all the tasty food I would consume the next day, and I planned on stuffing my face with every darn carb in sight.

"We'll start off with shrimp remoulade, then move on to a pleasant corn and crab bisque. For the main dish, I've got crawfish jambalaya with red beans. So far, so good?" Francois asked as he glanced over the rim of his glasses.

"It sounds delicious," Mama said.

"What's for dessert?" I asked.

"Ah, my favorite part of the meal!" Francois exclaimed. "Banana pudding with beignets."

With a groan, I rolled my eyes. "Oh, my gosh. I love beignets!"

"Excellent!" Francois said. "I love nothing more than to see a happy bride!"

"Thank you again for doing this for us," Mama said. "We really appreciate it."

"Of course, love," Francois replied, his pen poised over his notebook. "Now, what is the final head count? Has it changed at all?"

"No. We're still looking at right around thirty people," Mama said.

"Perfect," Francois replied as he made notes. "No change in the schedule, I hope?"

"No," I answered. "We exchange our vows at three and we eat at four. Dancing starts at five."

Francois glanced out the window and sighed. "I'm so honored to be included in this wonderful celebration, Tilly."

"We're glad to have you," I said, glancing at the clock.

My initial plan for the day had been to relax and wait for my best friend, Debbie, to arrive. Instead, I had to find a dress, and my anxiety levels increased by the minute.

"Well, I best be saying *au revoir*," Francois said, standing. "It's been lovely chatting with you ladies, but I have two weddings tomorrow, so I must bid you farewell. A busy twenty-four hours lie ahead of *moi*!"

We said our goodbyes, walked Francois to the door, and I headed into the kitchen in desperate need of more coffee. As I stood at the sink and poured a cup, I glanced through the window to find Hank and Derek coming around the side of the house with strings of lights. They both waved as I opened the screen door.

"Did they find the dress?" Derek asked.

I shook my head. "We're heading out in a few minutes to get a replacement."

Derek handed the lights to Hank, then took my hands in his. "I'd marry you in your pajamas. You don't need a dress if it's causing too much stress."

"Thanks, but you're going to be in a tux, and everyone else will be wearing their Sunday best. I *do* need a dress, Derek. I want our wedding to be perfect."

"All right. I'll see you when you get home."

I shut the door and sipped my coffee. "What are they doing with all the lights, Mama?"

"They're going to string them up over the deck for dancing tomorrow night," Mama said, placing her hand on my shoulder. "It will be like a thousand little stars above us. Won't that be gorgeous?"

"Wow. Yes, it will."

My heart warmed as I imagined swaying with Derek under the lights. I couldn't wait to marry him.

"When did you want to leave, honey?"

"Give me ten minutes to finish this coffee," I replied. "Then we'll go."

"I've got a list of stores for us to try," Mama said. "Don't worry. We'll find something."

WE WALKED through the French Quarter of New Orleans. I never tired of the Creole architecture and the Spanish and French influences. The mishmash of cultures and building styles probably would have resembled a mess anywhere else, but in New Orleans, it seemed to be the perfect combination and produce a magical feeling, as if the stories and legends of ghosts, vampires, and witches would suddenly come to life.

While the French Quarter was considered a tourist area, a few specialty shops could be found. Mama pulled me into a narrow doorway leading to an enclosed staircase.

"What's this place?" I asked.

"Her name's Madame Bouchard," she replied. "She's supposed to have a great selection of dresses."

The musty smell of old building filtered through the air as we climbed the stairs. We'd been to two stores so far, and my search had resulted in a bit goose egg. Frankly, I was ready to wear my pajamas. "I hope I find something I like. Debbie is supposed to be here soon."

"I'm sure we will, honey."

At the top of the stairs, we were met by a closed door. Mama knocked, then tried the handle.

"Come in!" a woman's voice sounded from inside.

Natural light filled the huge space. I heard footsteps but couldn't see anyone through the racks of dresses. Mama had been right—there shouldn't be any trouble with me finding a dress.

An African American woman emerged through all the silk and chiffon, a wide grin across her face.

She wore a green dress, her long braids piled high on top of her head. I pegged her to be my age.

"Welcome to my store!" she said, shaking Mama's hand, then mine, her voice thick with a southern accent. "What can I do to help?"

Mama glanced over her shoulder at me.

"I'm getting married tomorrow and I need a dress," I said.

"Tomorrow?" she asked, her smile fading. "Why in the world would you wait until the last moment to find a dress?"

"I flew in from California yesterday to get married at my parent's house," I replied. "The airline lost my dress."

Madame Bouchard shook her head while rubbing the bridge of her nose with her pointer finger. "Such a tragedy."

"Do you think you can help us?" Mama asked.

"Yes, I can," she replied eyeing me from head-to-toe. "We'll have to find something that's not going to require any alterations. What are you... a size six? Perhaps a four?"

I nodded, once again thrilled I'd lost all my weight.

"Okay, love. Follow me."

We pushed through the lace, beads, chiffon and

silk to an open area by the windows with two couches and a pedestal framed with a three-way mirror.

"Wait here," Madame Bouchard ordered, pointing to the couches. "Instead of you going through all the dresses, let me bring out the ones that I know will work in this particular emergency."

She disappeared into the fluff once again. My mother and I sat down.

"Such a lovely day," Mama said, glancing out the windows. The sunlight streaming in was almost blinding, but I nodded in agreement.

"Here we go," Madame Bouchard said as she emerged carrying a slew of dresses over her arm. "These will all fit you and not require any alterations. I'm certain of it."

I stood and hurried over as she hung them on the rack. The one with the rhinestone bodice definitely wasn't my style. Neither was the pencil skirt. I'd land on my face if I tried to walk in that one. I grabbed the one with the lace decolletage and walked over to the changing room while Madame Bouchard and Mama chatted.

The dress was pretty and I could walk in the big, flouncy skirt. Madame Bouchard hadn't lied when she said she'd find ones that would fit me. I couldn't imagine any alterations that needed to be done.

I pulled back the curtain and exited the dressing room. The two women quit talking and Mama gasped. "Oh, Tilly... you look beautiful!"

Madame Bouchard nodded. "Yes. The dress fits you well, but I can tell it's not the right one for you."

"How do you know that?" I asked as I stood on the platform and studied my reflection from all sides.

"You don't have that sparkle in your eye... the one that lets me know the dress has touched your soul."

I tried to recall a time when a piece of clothing had ever 'touched my soul,' and I was at a loss.

"Let's try another one that catches your fancy," Madame Bouchard said. "This one isn't it."

Three dresses later, her eyes lit up. "That's the one," she whispered.

I stood on the platform and spun around. The dress was simple—no ornaments or lace—and it fit as if it had been made for me.

"Tilly, I think she's right," Mama said. "Your soul is glowing. I can see it in your eyes."

With a grin, I nodded. It wasn't *my* wedding dress, but I did feel beautiful. "Yes, we've found it."

Relief swept through me. I had a dress, the

catering was set, and the backyard held a casual elegance. I was marrying the man I loved, the one who had stuck around and been so patient as I'd grown and flourished.

My wedding day would be perfect. There was nothing else that could go wrong... right?

CHAPTER 2

When Mama and I arrived back at her house, Debbie was sitting in the living room sipping tea and checking her phone.

"Derek told me what happened!" she said, hurrying to her feet and over to me. "My word, Tilly. What a horrible situation."

"We found another one," I said as we embraced. "It's going to be fine. The new dress looks great on me."

Derek came into the living room and gave me a quick kiss on the nose. "Everything go okay?"

"Yes, but I need to bring the dress into the house, so can you make yourself scarce? I don't want you to see it before our wedding."

He chuckled and squeezed my hand. "Of course.

Hank and I are going out here in a few minutes anyway. Debbie has already told us to scatter."

I glanced over at my friend. "What do you have up your sleeve?"

A sly grin slid over her lips. "Something for us ladies."

"Please tell me you didn't get a stripper," I groaned, shaking my head. "Please."

"Of course not!" Debbie exclaimed. "Who needs hunky men gyrating all over the place? I've got something even better!"

"What?"

"You'll find out," Debbie said with a wink. "You sit down and make yourself comfortable while I go scheme with your mom in the kitchen."

"I already have everything you asked for, Debbie," Mama said as the two linked arms. "We're all set."

Derek and I stared at each other a beat as I tried to muster some enthusiasm for whatever Debbie had concocted.

"I'm exhausted," I said. "I was really looking forward to us hanging out and watching television."

"No rest for the bride," Derek said as Hank thundered down the stairs.

"There's my girl!" he boomed. "Did you find a dress?"

"Yes."

"Excellent. "I'm taking Derek out for a bit so you ladies can do your thing."

"Do you happen to know what that 'thing' is?" I asked, hopeful that he'd spill the secret just because he loved me.

"Nope," Hank said, his smile widening, which indicated that he did indeed know exactly what Debbie had in store for me.

"Please tell me?"

"I can't, honey," Hank said, drawing me into an embrace. "If I did, they'd feed me to Irwin's friends. I've been sworn to secrecy."

Irwin was a gator that lived out back of my parent's home. I didn't really know if gators had friends or not, or if Mama and Debbie had made an empty threat. Irwin hadn't shown himself since we arrived, so maybe he was indeed hanging out with his friends.

"We better head out, son!" Hank said. "Let's go get some food and let these ladies get on with their night."

Derek and Hank walked out the front door and I sat down on the couch. Not much had changed in the room since I'd left home. The worn, brown leather sofa continued to cradled my body with perfection, my high school graduation picture still hung on the wall. Mama had told me she'd taken down all the wedding pictures of Tommy and me after he left me, and I hoped we'd get some great shots tomorrow. Getting married was exhausting, especially with the airline losing my dress and the stress that had come along with it. At least now I could relax. Everything was in place, and I just needed to attend, drink a little champagne, eat and say my vows.

"Here we go!" Debbie said, entering the living room with a tray. My stomach howled as I looked at all the baked goodies.

"Are those from your bakery?" I asked.

"Yes. Remember Carla was trying out new ways for me to accomplish sugar-free supremacy?"

I nodded. Debbie had visions of selling her baked goods worldwide, but she also didn't want to add a bunch of artificial preservatives to keep them fresh during shipping.

"Well, I think she found a way. I sent these two days before I left, and it seems like they're in perfect condition. We'll see how they taste."

"I've got some wine!" Mama said. She brought in a bottle and three glasses.

They sat on each side of me and Mama poured while Debbie set out some plates and forks.

"Here's to you, Tilly." Mama held up her glass. "I'm so thrilled you've found happiness."

"Me, too," Debbie agreed as we all clinked glasses. "Derek is a good guy, and lucky to have found you."

I took a sip of wine, then set down my glass. "Thanks. I'm thrilled you both are here with me."

The doorbell rang just as I took a bite of a strawberry goody. Mama and Debbie exchanged glances, both of them grinning, while I groaned.

"I'll get it," Debbie said, hurrying to the front door.

While I fully expected a chiseled man greased up like a pig, surprise washed through me when an older, frail woman, who couldn't have weighed a hundred pounds soaking wet, entered. When she smiled, I noted her two front teeth were missing.

"Hello, everyone," she said as she set down her bag. "It's so lovely to be here."

I glanced over at Debbie, then at Mama. Both just grinned and I still had no idea who sat in the living room.

"This is Edna," Debbie said. "I spent weeks trying to find the best psychic in Louisiana, and here she is. Edna is going to enlighten us about our futures."

Psychic ability was always something I didn't know whether to believe in or not. Sometimes I heard stories of readings that turned out to be absolutely true, but then I'd watched documentaries on so-called psychics and learned about the ways they ask questions to get the answers they needed.

Edna intrigued me, and I actually looked forward to the evening. Much better than a stripper.

"Would you like some wine, Edna?" Mama asked.

"No, thank you," she replied. "Alcohol diminishes my abilities." She glanced at the three of us, her gaze finally landing on my mother. "I'd like to do a reading for you first. Your aura is very positive and bright."

"Oh, how exciting!" Mama said, standing. "What do we do?"

"If you could grab two chairs from the kitchen, we can set them up facing each other right here," Edna said.

Mama and Debbie hurried into the kitchen and returned with the chairs, placing them as Edna had instructed.

The older woman moved to one of the chairs and told Mama to sit in the other. Then she pulled some candles out of her bag and set them on the table.

After lighting them, she asked Debbie to turn out the lights.

My heart skipped a beat as Edna closed her eyes and took Mama's hands in hers. "Take some deep breaths with me while I attempt to connect to the spirit world."

Mama did as instructed and a heavy silence fell over the room. Long moments passed before the psychic spoke again.

"I see so much love around you," she finally whispered. "You've found your soulmate, your other half. It has taken many life cycles, but you've finally been connected."

Debbie and I exchanged glances. Mama and Hank were definitely two peas in a pod.

"I see a few rough patches ahead for you... and his name is Hank. Is that correct, dear? That's what the spirits are telling me, but I'm not sure if they are referring to his name in this life or a previous one."

"Yes, it's Hank," Mama said.

"These times coming... they will be difficult, but it's important to remember that love you share for one another. It will keep you bonded, and it will carry over into your next life."

"Can you tell me what these rough patches are?" Mama asked.

Edna shook her head. "I don't know if it's illness, financial worries, or something else. The spirits won't elaborate. They just want you to stay the course, to remember the eternal love that brought you together."

Tears welled in Mama's eyes as she nodded. "I will. That man drives me crazy at times, but I do love him very much."

The psychic opened her eyes and smiled. "Men have a tendency to do that." She then turned to Debbie and me, her gaze finally settling on my friend. "You're next, dear. The spirits are whispering loudly about the woman with the red hair."

"I hope that's a good thing," Debbie muttered as she rose to her feet, then took the chair Mama had vacated.

Edna took her hands and once again closed her eyes. "My goodness," she said after a moment. "So much energy coming from you. It pulsates around you like a heartbeat."

I snickered as I drank my wine. No truer words had ever been uttered.

"Besides the vitality, I see wealth surrounding you, dear. You're on the precipice of a new beginning for yourself. You've worked so hard and it's about to pay off."

Debbie grinned and bounced a little in her chair. "I have been busting my butt for years."

"Shh... quiet, please. I'm getting other messages," Edna said. "The spirits are trying to communicate something else."

Long moments passed while the spirits talked with Edna, and I wondered what they sounded like. Did they whisper in her ear? Talk in tongues? Puzzles? Or was the communication like having a normal conversation?

"The windfall you will experience... I see someone else involved. A very beautiful Black woman. Carly? Karen? Maybe Candy?"

"That's Carla," Debbie said. "What about her?"

"It's imperative that you give proper accolades where they are due, that you compensate her well. If this is not done, the universe will destroy your wealth or your ability to generate it. You must appease the spirits and act in a fair manner."

"I'd never screw over Carla," Debbie said, her voice indignant and irritable. "She's not only my friend, but a huge part of my business now."

"Good," Edna replied. "You must keep the balance."

"No worries there."

"Wait! There's something else," Edna said. "I see...

what is this? How very interesting. I see love in your not-so-distant future, dear."

Debbie rolled her eyes. "I don't have a man in my life by design. I don't want to fight over the remote or pick up dirty socks. I'm married to my business."

"Ah... well, I'm afraid someone is going to catch your interest, and possibly your heart." Edna opened her eyes and smiled. "Allow it to happen. Embrace what the universe has to offer you."

Debbie stood and nodded, her face pinched in confusion. She'd always sworn she'd never settle down, and I'd never doubted her. Perhaps Edna was full entertainment, not truths.

"Now you, dear," Edna said, raising an arthritic finger in my direction. "Come sit with me."

I took a deep breath and walked around the coffee table. Edna's fingers felt cold as she grasped my hands.

As she settled in, her eyes closed and I studied her. Her wrinkled face flinched and pinched as if she were having a conversation with someone, one she didn't fully understand.

"That can't be right," Edna muttered. "What are you trying to tell me?"

Her lips pursed together and her eyebrows furrowed. I became incredibly uncomfortable at the long stretch of silence and tried to remind myself Edna's presence was for entertainment purposes only. We had no idea if what she proclaimed would come true.

"What do you see?" Mama asked, her voice tense.

"I see... I see a long happy life ahead of you, dear," Edna murmured. "But there is a darkness as well."

"What's that?" I asked, my stomach flipping and flopping with nerves when I glanced over at Mama and Debbie.

"Usually, it means... chaos."

"Chaos?"

"Yes," Edna said, abruptly letting go of my hands. "Chaos. I'm sorry dear, but I must take my leave."

Debbie stood and reached for her purse, then paid Edna and showed her to the door.

I hadn't moved when the lights went on. Edna had been in such a hurry, she'd left her candles.

The light mood had been replaced with heavy dread.

"Wasn't that silly," Mama said with a laugh. "Fun, but absolute silliness. No one can predict the future."

"Exactly," Debbie agreed. "Like any man is ever going to hold my interest."

Pasting on a smile, I carried one of the chairs Edna had used back into the kitchen.

Chaos. Bedlam. Disorder. Call it what you want, it still meant things weren't going to go my way.

"Just keep everything normal until after the wedding," I whispered under my breath, hoping that any lingering spirits would hear me. "Please, just until after the wedding."

But for some reason, I had the distinct impression no one was listening.

CHAPTER 3

$\mathcal{M}$y wedding day.

I never thought I'd be standing in my parents' house with a horrible case of wedding day jitters, especially after Tommy left me and I had no intention of ever looking for love again. However, it had found me, and I had the most amazing husband-to-be.

From the upstairs bedroom, I watched as the guests filtered into the backyard, everyone wearing dresses and suits. Mama and Hank greeted everyone warmly with hugs, kisses, and a glass of champagne. Around the side of the house, Francois' crew worked to prepare our meal. They'd carried in tables and covered silver buffet tins earlier, and my mouth watered at the thought of all that amazing Creole food we would be eating.

A nice, light cloud cover had settled above us to protect everyone from the sun's unrelenting rays, the downside being the humidity had risen. My hair had no hope of lying flat, so Debbie had braided it and set it in a fancy design on top of my head.

A knock sounded at the bedroom door and Debbie hurried over to answer it. My cousin, Bernadette, stood on the other side. We both screamed in delight as she rushed in. After I moved to Louisiana when I was ten, we'd become fast friends, but had lost touch when I'd gone to California to marry Tommy and she'd left for Arizona after inheriting her grandmother's house. Tears welled in my eyes I was so happy to see her.

"I'm so glad you could come, Bernie!"

"Oh, I wouldn't miss this for the world," she said as we embraced. Then I introduced her to Debbie, and I could tell they would click, too. "Let's have a toast!"

I hugged my cousin again. "No, thanks. I don't want to be drunk for my wedding."

"One glass isn't going to make you drunk," Debbie said, rolling her eyes as she poured three glasses. "It'll help calm your nerves."

"Oh! I love champagne!" Bernie exclaimed. "All in moderation, of course."

"Of course," I said, taking the flute from Debbie. The three of us clinked glasses.

"I wish Carla could be here to see this," Debbie said, her eyes becoming misty.

"Me, too. It's unfortunate Mac couldn't get time off."

"Such a shame," Debbie said, pulling out her phone from her pocket. "But I promised her lots of pictures, so say cheese!"

The three of us placed our heads together and Debbie snapped a couple of photos.

Instead of a dress, Debbie had decided to wear a tuxedo—a pink tuxedo, to be exact, along with a white ruffled shirt. Frankly, she looked adorable.

"You're so beautiful, Tilly," Debbie said. "And honestly, I think I may like this dress better than the old one."

"Really?"

"Oh, yes. It's simple and fits you well."

"It's super pretty," Bernie agreed, tucking a lock of her black hair behind her ear. "You look cuter than wings on a June bug."

"Well, thank you," I replied, turning back to the window, smiling at the fact she had lost her southern accent while living in Arizona, but kept the colloqui-alisms. "I wonder where the pastor is. We're supposed to exchange our vows at three—in five minutes."

"Do you want me to go down and ask your mom about it?" Debbie asked. "Perhaps he's running late or something."

"Yes, if you could."

"Yes, ma'am. Be back in a flash."

I stared out the window and sipped my cham-pagne while Bernie came up beside me and wrapped her arm around me. She rested her head on my shoul-der. Flashes of us catching frogs and running through the rain flew through my mind, along with visions of her telling me about her first kiss at sixteen and us saying goodbye when I'd moved to California and she to Arizona. Why I hadn't kept in touch, I didn't fully understand, because I loved her like a sister. Perhaps I'd been embarrassed that Tommy had left me?

Debbie came into view and pulled my mom to the side. "I like her," Bernadette said as we watched the two talk.

"I do, too. She's become one of my good friends in California. How's Arizona?" I asked, laying my hand on her cheek.

"It's awesome, Tilly. Living in Sedona is magical. I hope you and Derek will come visit soon."

"We will," I promised. "How long are you staying in Louisiana?"

"I'm staying with Daddy and leaving in a few days," she said, referring to Hank's brother, who I noted sitting at one of the tables outside, checking his watch.

"Let's make sure to spend some time together after the wedding," I said. "I've missed you."

"Same here, girl. Same here."

As Mama pulled her phone from her pocket, her forehead creased in worry. She dialed as Debbie looked up at me, grinned, then waved.

After Mama hung up, she and Debbie talked for a few minutes, then they both came into the house. I stared at my bedroom door waiting for the bad news while my anxiety levels soared, hoping Pastor Matthew was just late.

"Something isn't right," Bernie whispered.

"Yes," I said as the knock sounded on the door. "Come in!"

"Hi, honey," Mama said as she entered a moment later. "How are you?"

"Where is he?"

"Well, Pastor Matthew been in a car accident," Mama said, wringing her hands.

"Oh, my goodness!" I exclaimed. "Is he okay?"

"Yes, it's nothing serious, but I'm afraid he won't be coming today."

I sank to the bed and held my head in my hands. "So... we won't be getting married."

"You can get married!" Debbie said, grabbing my laptop from the dresser. "Give me five minutes." As she flipped it open and sat down in a chair, I wondered what she was up to. "Don't you worry," she muttered while her fingers flew over the keyboard. "I've got this one."

"What's she doing?" Bernie whispered. "Does she know another pastor in the area?"

"I don't think so," I replied. But honestly, with Debbie, anything was possible.

About a minute passed and Debbie set down the computer and stood. "And here I am! An ordained minister ready to marry my best friend!"

Mama, Bernie, and I exchanged glances. Their faces pinched in confusion.

"What in the heck are you talking about, Debbie?" Bernie asked.

"I've just become an ordained minister through the internet and I can marry Tilly!"

"Are you kidding me?" I asked. "Is that even legal?"

"Oh, my goodness," Bernie exclaimed. "You *are* getting hitched!"

"You will be legally married," Debbie said, taking my hand and pulling me from the bed. "I may be a little rusty on the vows, but I can marry you right now."

"Oh, my word," Mama muttered, staring at me with wide eyes. "Tilly, are you okay with this? We can postpone the wedding... or have a fake ceremony and take you down to the courthouse. I don't—"

"Yes, let's do it!" I said. The thought of Debbie legally marrying me tickled me through and through. What a fun story to tell!

"This is so cute!" Bernie squealed.

"Should we ask Derek?" Mama said. "He may not be comfortable with the idea."

"Oh, definitely," Debbie said. "I'll wait here with Tilly while you go find him. I'm sure he'll be fine with it, but we should confirm."

"I'll come with you," Bernie said, and they hurried from the room as I glanced out the window again. Derek stood where we should have been saying our vows at that very moment, his face a mask of confusion.

"He probably thinks I've left him at the altar," I muttered. "I can't believe this."

Mama strode over to him and whispered in his ear. He nodded, then glanced up at the window, a huge grin on his face.

"Looks like he's fine with the plan," Debbie said. "Grab that bouquet and let's get you hitched, as Bernie so eloquently put it!"

We hurried out of the bedroom and down the stairs, my heart thundering and my hand shaking as we met Hank by the sliding glass door.

"Wait here until I give you the signal," Debbie instructed, stepping outside and shutting the door behind her.

"Do you know what the signal is?" Hank asked, threading my arm through his. "Your mom just shared the plan with me."

"I have no idea. I guess we'll figure that out when we see it."

"Most likely," Hank said, patting my hand. "You're making the right decision here, Tilly. Derek's a good man. I'm happy for you."

Our gazes locked and Hank's eyes misted over. He moved his stare back to the window. "Quit looking at me," he said with a chuckle. "You're going to make me cry like a baby."

I glanced out the window at Debbie, who gave us two thumbs up.

Hank opened the door and all the guests turned to us. I listened for the music that should have been playing—*What a Wonderful World* by Louis Armstrong—but heard nothing except the rustling of my dress as I walked.

So the music hadn't worked... big deal. This day wasn't about a stereo malfunction. It was about Derek and me beginning a new life.

Derek's gaze never left me as we approached. When Hank handed me off to him, he whispered, "You look really pretty."

"Thank you."

Debbie cleared her throat as she studied the rooftop, her brow furrowed in concentration. "Dearly beloved, we are gathered here today on this very happy occasion to witness the marriage of Derek York and Tilly Bordeaux, two of my favorite people in this big, wide world."

Derek and I exchanged glances and he squeezed my palm.

"So, here we go," Debbie said, her gaze meeting mine, then Derek's. "Derek, do you take Tilly and promise to love her and cherish her, to not take advantage of her delicate heart, to help with the dishes, not leave dirty socks in the bathroom and help with the feeding of the chickens?"

I pursed my lips together to keep from giggling. Debbie obviously had no idea what the traditional vows should be, but I appreciated her making it up as she went along.

Laughter titillated from the crowd as Derek said, "I do. "

"And Tilly," Debbie said, her face serious. "Do you promise to love Derek in sickness and health, for richer or poorer—although I don't foresee any money troubles in your future with his bank account —and to not get upset even if he breaks his vows not to leave dirty socks on the floor?"

Derek and I both burst out laughing, as did our guests. Grinning, Debbie arched an eyebrow, waiting for my answer.

"I do," I said.

The traditional vows had flown out the window, but marriage was about the small things. Like dirty socks, dishes, and remotes. It was about compromise and finding ways to—

An ear-piercing scream sounded from behind us and startled me so badly, I dropped my bouquet.

We turned to find our guests scattering, racing every which way while chairs toppled over. One man bumped into me and sent me butt-first to the grass. Derek quickly helped me up and when everyone had cleared, I saw the issue.

Irwin.

I narrowed my gaze on the gator, absolutely furious. He hadn't shown up since I arrived, but now chose my wedding day to make an appearance and scare everyone senseless?

"Irwin!" Hank yelled. "What the heck?"

The gator kept sauntering toward Derek and me, and we slowly backed up.

"I was beginning to wonder if he was real, or if your dad was telling more stories," Derek muttered. "Is that thing going to bite us? Is he honestly a pet?"

Hank raced into the house and emerged a few seconds later with a bag of marshmallows. He chucked one at Irwin, who stopped his advances and ate it.

"Dang it, boy!" Hank yelled. "We're in the middle of a wedding!"

Irwin turned to Hank, who threw him another marshmallow.

"Let's get out of here," Debbie said.

To my knowledge, Irwin had never attacked anyone. Not Hank, not my mom. But he'd never been surrounded by so many strangers, either.

The three of us hustled to the side of the house where Francois and his employees were setting up the food.

"What's going on?" Francois asked. "It's not time for the food!"

"Irwin decided to show up," Debbie replied. "Dang gator chased everyone away."

"*Mon Dieu!*" Francois exclaimed. "What a shame!"

"What a mess," I muttered.

"At least we have wonderful delicacies to feast on," Francois said, placing his hand on my shoulder. "Come and see the beautiful dishes."

I followed him over, disappointed that we hadn't even gotten through our vows. Between the dress, the music, the pastor's car accident, and now Irwin, I wondered if the universe was telling me I shouldn't be married. At least the meal where I would drown my sorrows should be delicious.

"Look at this!" Francois exclaimed, lifting the silver lid with flourish. "Take in the gorgeous meal I've prepared for you!"

He stared at me expectantly with a large grin as I studied the dish. "That's not what we ordered," I said, thoroughly confused. "That's a pile of noodles."

Francois smile faded as he followed my gaze. He pulled the lids off the rest of the buffet tins while whispering a few curses. "What the heck happened here?!"

When he dropped each lid, more pasta was revealed.

"Kara! Kara!" he yelled. "What is this?" His assistant, a woman about my age with blonde hair, came running over. Her eyes widened when she realized what lay on the buffet table.

"This is supposed to go to the Italian wedding!" Francois yelled.

"I took the truck George told me to!" she said, tears welling in her eyes. "George gave me the keys and the address!"

"We need to check such things!" Francois screamed, his eyes bulging while his face turned beet red.

"I thought George had checked it since he was the one who gave me the keys!"

Pursing my lips, I stared at the noodles. I had wanted to load my face with a bunch of carbs, but not noodles—rather, the tasty Creole stuff that burst with flavor and the sweet reminder that I got married in Louisiana.

Thunder rumbled in the distance, which didn't surprise me in the least. Of course, it would rain on my wedding day.

Francois and Kara continued to yell at each other —something about the Italian family being in the witness protection program for turning on the mob and providing the government with information on one of the bosses. They'd have Francois' head on a serving platter.

"Are you okay?" Derek asked, wrapping his arm around my shoulder.

I glanced down at my grass-stained dress. Car doors slammed out in front as people left, and I didn't blame them. The day had been a disaster, and I recalled Edna had spoken of my darkness, of the chaos.

She'd hit that one on the head.

"No," I replied. "I think I'll get some champagne."

I left Derek, Francois, and Kara while Debbie followed me around to the backyard. I had no tears of anger or sorrow. I simply felt numb.

Irwin was still lying in the middle of the grass surrounded by tables and chairs while Hank tried to coax him back to the water.

Rain began to fall.

"Tilly!" Mama said, running toward me. "Honey, we can fix this!"

"No, we can't, Mama," I said with a sigh. "Right

now, I just want some champagne and to get out of this dress."

As I went upstairs to change, I felt nothing. Anger was nowhere to be found. Instead, I accepted everything that had happened. My lost dress. The pastor's car accident. Irwin showing up at the worst time. The rain. More noodles than I could ever want to eat. It seemed to be the way my life went. Chaos. I slipped out of my dress and into some jeans and a sweatshirt.

"Tilly?" Derek's voice filtered through from the other side of the door. "Can I come in?"

"Yes," I called.

Drenched from head-to-toe, he carried a glass of champagne and handed it to me. "What a mess."

"I know. At this point, I'm just accepting it," I replied, then took a long drink. "I think I'll go down and help Francois and Kara clean up."

"Francois left, but Kara's still here."

"Okay, I'll go down and give her a hand."

"Maybe later we can talk about everything?"

"Sure. Of course."

After a few moments, I finished my champagne while Derek changed out of his tuxedo, then I trotted down the stairs and out to the backyard. Irwin had moved under a tree and seemed fairly content. Glancing over my shoulder every few steps, I was thankful he didn't move.

When I rounded the corner, I noted almost everything had been cleaned up. The buffet tins were packed away, but the tables remained in place. The catering van sat running at the gate leading to the front yard.

As I strode over through the rain, I hoped Kara didn't get fired over my wedding—I'd feel terrible. Later tonight I'd call Francois and have him promise me she'd continue employment with him. It wasn't her fault that "chaos" followed me.

Kara sat in the driver's seat of the van, her face turned away from me. I tapped on the window, but she didn't move, so I rapped my knuckles again.

I pulled open the door and gasped. Because of my height, I couldn't see her chest—just her face through the glass. But now that I had a full view of her, the sight of a knife sticking out of her sternum shocked me more than I could have ever imagined.

CHAPTER 4

The first responders showed up moments later, as did the sheriff, who corralled us back into the house. Derek, Debbie, and I sat on the couch, while Mama and Hank shared the loveseat. My mother stared off into space, seemingly shell-shocked, while Debbie tapped away at her phone, giving Carla blow-by-blow updates of the utter disaster my wedding day had become.

"I can't believe someone was killed at my home," Mama murmured. "This has been a horrific day."

"Dang right it has," Hank said, taking a sip from his flask. "We worked so hard to make this day perfect, and it all went to heck."

Derek took my hand in his and squeezed it. I smiled through my simmering anger at the whole situation, almost feeling as if my wedding had somehow been targeted by someone who didn't want to see me married. The idea seemed absurd, but I couldn't shake it.

A few moments later, the sheriff entered through the front door.

"Well, she's dead," he said, removing his hat.

I shut my eyes for a brief moment and bit my tongue to keep my sarcasm to myself.

"My name's Sheriff Marvin Brewer," he continued. "I'll be handling this murder."

Debbie smiled and waved while Derek and I simply stared at him.

"It's nice to see you again, Marv," Hank said as he walked over and stuck out his hand. "It's been a while."

"Yes sir, it has."

The two men shook hands and the tension in the room slowly escalated while they stared each other down. Did the two have history?

Their palms finally dropped and Hank returned to his place by Mama.

"I'll need to get statements from all of you," Sheriff Brewer stated. "Mind if I use your kitchen to do so? I'll call you in one by one."

"Help yourself," Mama said. "I'll make some coffee."

"Thank you, ma'am," he replied, his gaze softening as he studied her. "I can take your statement while you do so."

Mama and the sheriff went into the kitchen and I glanced over at Hank. "What's the story? It seems you two hate each other."

Hank nodded. "There's some bad blood there, but he's been a good cop, so I'm sure he can keep his feelings about me out of the investigation and remain impartial."

"What happened?" Derek asked.

Hank gazed over his shoulder for a moment, then lowered his voice. "When Tilly and her mom first moved here, old Marv in there had eyes for Jennifer. I came in and swooped her off her feet. He's never forgiven me."

"That was over twenty years ago!" I exclaimed.

"Yes, it was. But some wounds to the heart never heal. He's hated me ever since, and I think he still loves Jennifer."

Mama and the sheriff talked in low tones so we couldn't fully hear the conversation. My stomach howled in hunger as I sipped more champagne and we all sat in silence. I was completely and utterly done with the day.

My mind kept going back to Kara. Had she been married? Kids? Who had taken her life, and more importantly, why? Had the murder been senseless, or had the woman been caught up in something horrible and nefarious? And why had the killer chosen my parents' yard to end her life?

Mama hurried out from the kitchen and sat down next to Hank, then grabbed his flask and took a long drink while Hank massaged her shoulder. Whatever had been said between her and the sheriff hadn't sat well.

"I'll talk to Tilly next," Marv said from the archway.

My track record with police interviews had been shaky at best, either steered by fear or irritation. With a sigh, I stood and followed him into the kitchen, determined to remain professional and aloof.

I sat down across the kitchen table from him and finished off my champagne while I studied his weathered face. The deep grooves indicated he'd spent plenty of time in the Louisiana sun while his thinning blonde hair stayed plastered to his forehead despite him removing his hat.

"Do you remember me from your childhood?" he asked, not meeting my gaze while jotting down notes on his pad of paper.

"No," I replied as I tried to read his chicken scratch. "I don't remember ever meeting you."

"We actually were introduced three times," he said with a sigh, then set down his pen. His hard brown gaze met mine and I immediately knew we weren't going to be friends. "You don't remember?"

"Sorry, no."

He chuckled and shook his head. "It doesn't surprise me. You were a needy thing. I think you were around eleven or so... clinging to your mom like a lifeline. Very self-absorbed."

I smiled and nodded, not dignifying him with a response. Self-absorbed would be an excellent way to describe a girl who had recently lost her father and had moved to a new state. Probably frightened and unsure of the future had something do with the behavior as well. "What questions do you have for me, Mr. Brewer?"

"That's sheriff to you," he said, his gaze narrowed.

"Of course. My apologies."

However he wanted me to address him, I would, just to finish the interview sooner rather than later.

"Tell me about the day."

"It was awful," I said without batting an eye. "Simply awful."

"You're saying that about your wedding?"

"Oh, yes."

After explaining everything from the second my plane had landed and I realized the airline had lost my wedding dress, to the missing music, Irwin's appearance, the rain, the noodles, and then discovering the body, he paled.

"It sure seems like someone didn't want this wedding to happen," he murmured as he made notes.

I had considered that angle, but it didn't make any sense. No one controlled nature—Irwin and the rain—but I supposed someone could have instigated the rest of the day's events. "Maybe," I muttered with a shrug, but I highly doubted it.

"What do you think of your fiancé?" Sheriff Brewer asked. "I hate to ask, but do you think he *wants* to marry you?"

I stared at the man for a brief moment, then nodded. "Yes. I'm sure."

Derek had been given plenty of opportunities to run from me, including in the first moment we met where I'd threatened to beat him over the head with a baseball bat. If he didn't want to marry me, he could easily have disappeared from my life many times.

"How long have y'all known each other?"

"It will be a year in July."

"That's a quickie marriage," he replied, meeting my gaze. "You knocked up or something?"

"Is that really any of your business?" I shot back.

"Yes. There was a dead woman in the yard and it's my job to find the killer, so it's all my business."

Well, he had a point there, but he didn't need to be such a jerk. "No, I'm not pregnant," I muttered through gritted teeth. "There's this thing called love. That's all it is. There's no other reason."

"It's the right reason to get hitched," he said. "You said you flew in. Where are you living?"

"It's a small town called Oak Peak in California."

"Why did you come all the way out here to get married?" he asked, his brow furrowed in confusion.

"We wanted to get married at my parents' home," I replied. "We thought it would be a nice setting with the grass and trees leading down to the water. They also had a lot of friends they wanted to invite who hadn't been able to attend my first wedding."

"Your first wedding?"

"Yes. I was married before. My husband left me."

"What was his name?"

I stared at him a beat before answering. "What does that have to do with figuring out who killed Kara?"

"Just looking at all angles," he said. "I like to accumulate a pile of information and sift through it. I never know what's important and what isn't."

Fair enough. "Tommy Donner. He's married with two kids and lives in New River, about thirty miles away from Oak Peak."

"Okay. How long are you in town?"

I shrugged. "We're supposed to leave on Wednesday."

"If you could stay a bit later, I'd appreciate it," the sheriff said. "I have a feeling I'm going to be wrapping this one up darn quick, but not as quick as Wednesday."

"I'll ask Derek if he's okay with that," I said. "I'll let you know."

Sheriff Brewer smiled and set down his pen. "It's not a request, Tilly. I'd hate to have to arrest you on suspicion of murder in order to keep you in town."

Could he do that? I had half a mind to head home tonight in order to find out. However, I did want to be helpful in catching Kara's killer. "When you put it that way, we'll stay a few days longer. I do have to get back to work, though."

"What's your job?"

"I'm a reporter for the Tri-Town Times, the local paper in our area."

He pursed his lips as he nodded. "Good for you. I'm not usually one who likes the press, but it's a noble profession if one can remain unbiased in their writing."

My stomach growled again, reminding me I hadn't eaten anything throughout the day. Derek had mentioned ordering a pizza after the police interviews, but according to my hunger pangs, sooner rather than later would be best.

"Are we done here?" I asked, getting to my feet.

"Yes. Thanks for your time."

He followed me out to the living room and called in Debbie.

"Did everything go okay?" Derek asked.

"Fine, but I really need to eat. Do you think we can order that pizza now?"

"I was thinking the same thing. One pie isn't going to cut it. Maybe two?"

"Better make it three," Hank said. "I'm hungrier than a bear coming out of hibernation."

"We should order four just to be safe," Derek said, picking up his phone. After he placed the order— one large sausage, a large pepperoni, a chicken and spinach with white sauce and a vegetarian—he set it back down. "Twenty minutes."

"That's fast," I said.

"Thankfully, yes. I'm about to pull the leather off the sofa and chow down," Derek said with a chuckle.

We had all been looking forward to an amazing wedding feast. Perhaps tomorrow we'd venture out to a Creole restaurant and order all the goodies we had missed out on.

Another hour passed while the sheriff conducted his interviews. The pizzas arrived, and we scarfed them down like feral dogs. When Hank emerged from the kitchen followed by the sheriff, we all stared at him expectantly.

"Here's what I have so far," Sheriff Brewer said as he glanced at his notebook. "Hank and Derek, you two were the last to see Kara alive. Tilly, you found the body."

We all exchanged glances and a sick sensation settled in my stomach, but I wasn't sure if it was from the pizza or what the sheriff was saying.

"Based on the information you've provided me, I do believe the killer is sitting right here in this room."

Mama gasped while Hank grabbed another slice

of pizza. Debbie rolled her eyes and my gaze slid over to Derek.

"That's ridiculous," Debbie scoffed. "No one here killed anyone, especially Kara. There were dozens of people at the wedding who could have offed her. Are you looking at any of them? What about someone coming in off the street? A serial killer who just had to have his fix for blood?"

Brewer smiled and nodded. "An excellent attempt at deflection, Debbie. I'll take into consideration all of your theories, as well as what the evidence on the body says, and find the guilty party. I'm convinced it will be one of you. Don't anyone think about leaving town."

He let himself out and none of us moved.

Not only had I not been married and someone had been killed at my wedding, now those I loved the most were all suspects.

I could only find one way to prove to the sheriff he was wrong: I had to find the killer myself.

All of the tables and chairs, as well as the sound equipment for the wedding, had been rented. The next day, Derek and Hank worked to break down everything outside for pickup while Mama, Debbie, Bernie and me supervised. Well, we drank coffee and watched them pack up the wedding that never happened, and I was so thrilled Bernie had come by. After the ceremony debacle, I had been afraid she'd stay away for good.

Somewhere in the night I'd accepted the fate of my wedding. I wasn't really sad or angry about any of it, but I was terribly upset about Kara's death. I couldn't think of anything else… besides the fact the sheriff seemed to have one of my family members in his crosshairs.

"That sheriff is almost as stupid as ours is at home," Debbie muttered. "I can't believe he thinks we killed Kara."

"I've been thinking about that," I replied. "Francois was furious with her. Late last night, I recalled him screaming at her about the Italian wedding and how they were under witness protection from the mob. Apparently, the family snitched or something like that. They were expecting huge plates of pasta and their wedding was ruined as well with the Creole food."

"Are you thinking they took their revenge out on poor Kara?" Bernie asked.

"Perhaps," I said with a shrug. "I'm just tossing ideas around."

"There were also about forty or fifty people here yesterday, including Francois' staff. Any of them could have been responsible," Debbie said, then set down her cup. "I've got an appointment with one of the local bakeries here in a bit about them carrying my sugar free line. I'll catch up with you two later, okay?"

"Of course," Mama said. "Drive carefully, honey."

"'Bye, Debbie," Bernie and I called in unison.

"Later, taters."

Mama let out a long sigh. "What's on the agenda today, girls?" she asked.

"I'd like to talk to Francois," I said. "Can you give me his address so I can go meet him?"

"Sure, but let me go with you, okay? Either that, or take Bernie."

"I can't," Bernie said, setting her mug in the sink. "I've got to get home and help Daddy clean the fish he caught this morning."

Crinkling my nose, I was glad I wasn't in Bernie's shoes. Cleaning out fish guts was not my forte. "All right, Mama," I said with a shrug. "If you want to come with me, that's fine."

"When do you want to leave?"

"Well, let me get my shoes on and we can take off."

"Sounds good. I'll go ask Derek and Hank if they want to join us. I think I have an idea of the answer because Hank never wants to go anywhere, but I'll ask to be sure."

When I came downstairs, Mama had her purse in hand. Bernie and I said our goodbyes and she left.

"Are the boys coming?" I asked.

"No," she replied, shaking her head. "But Derek asked you to go out to the backyard before we leave."

I opened the sliding door and noted Irwin

basking in the sun where all the tables had been. Hank and Derek each sat on a banquet chair drinking a soda, their gazes fixated on the gator. I loved that my stepdad and Derek had become so close in such a short period of time and that my parents had welcomed him with open arms.

When he saw me, Derek stood and walked over.

"Why are you going to see Francois today?" he asked, taking my palm in his.

"Well, the sheriff thinks that one of us killed Kara, and we can all agree that isn't true."

He pursed his lips and nodded. "Are you actively looking for a killer, Tilly?"

"Don't you think I should?"

"Not really. How are you going to explain nosing around in other people's business? Before, you had your job as a cover. What about now?"

"Beats me," I said with a sigh. "But I'm certain I don't want any of us to get caught up in the legal system for a crime we didn't commit."

"The sheriff did seem pretty set on sending one of us away for the murder."

"That bothered me, Derek," I replied. "And he also made it clear we couldn't leave town because he was going to wrap up the investigation quickly. He's really focused on us, and it doesn't sit well with me.

It reminds me of another law enforcement officer we've come to know all too well."

Derek nodded and crossed his arms over his chest. "I better call Steven Blackburn. He probably can't practice in Louisiana, but maybe he knows someone who can help us in case the sheriff does decide to pull us in."

Steven Blackburn was Derek's attorney, a hulk of a man who, judging by his looks, should have been dominating a professional wrestling ring, not practicing law.

"That's a really good idea," I said. "I'm sure he can help us out. It will be nice knowing we have someone in our corner even if we don't need him."

"And hopefully we won't. With any luck, there will be an arrest made before any of us get hauled in."

"And that's why I'm going to talk to Francois," I said. "Someone wanted to kill Kara and I'm going to find out who."

"Be careful, Tilly."

"Always."

"And Tilly?"

"Yes?"

"I still want to marry you," he said with a grin. "I meant it when I said I'd marry you if you were wearing your pajamas. If Debbie can do the ceremony, maybe we should think about having a small one at some point? Just you, me, Debbie and your parents?"

With a smile, I squeezed his hand. "What about Irwin?"

"He can come too this time," Derek replied with a chuckle.

"I want that so much, too, Derek, and I love your idea. But let's make sure none of us are going to prison first, okay?"

"Yes, ma'am."

WHEN WE ARRIVED AT FRANCOIS' house, he opened the door as we strode up the walkway.

"How do you know where he lives?" I asked my mom.

"He goes to my church and we've gathered here for some charity projects."

Mama had never been religious once we moved to Louisiana, but she had recently found a church she enjoyed. Personally, I think she'd joined more for the social aspect than for the religious one, although she had always considered herself very spiritual.

I nodded while I waved and smiled. As we drew closer, I could see Francois' disheveled clothes and hair, while deep purple bags hung under his red-rimmed eyes. The man appeared to be a hot mess. His mustache still hung a little crooked on his upper lip, so I assumed it was indeed real.

"Oh, Jennifer! Tilly! Please, come in! I'm so happy for the company!"

He hugged my mom and squeezed my hand as we entered his townhome. Done in greens and blues, I found the living room space quite relaxing.

"Sit down, sit down," he said. "I'm making some tea. Would either of you care for any? It's my own blend of vanilla and hibiscus, and quite soothing on the nerves."

"It sounds wonderful, Francois," Mama said. "I'd love a cup."

"I'll take one as well," I replied. "Do you have any cream?"

"Of course, love. Be back in a two-step jiffy!"

Mama and I settled in and waited. As I studied his house, I realized it was far cleaner and more organized than mine would ever be. Even the tomes in the bookcase were sorted by genre, then author. My own books stood in piles two feet high next to my bed. I couldn't find a speck of dust on any surface, while in my house, it was more the norm than not. Not an animal hair to be found on the sofa or floating through the air.

Suddenly, I missed Tinker and Belle with such ferocity, it brought tears to my eyes. I could have really used some cuddles from them—my first emotion since I realized my wedding had been ruined.

Francois returned moments later with a silver tea tray and matching cups. I quickly gathered myself as he poured from the decanter, lifting and lowering it with dramatic finesse. His flair carried over to every part of his life, even tea.

"Oh, this is nice," Mama said after taking a sip. "Thank you."

"We all need our nerves soothed after yesterday," Francois said. "*Mon Dieu.* How horrible. I feel absolutely awful about everything and I'm thoroughly sick over the tragic fate Kara met."

There was no time like the present to discuss murder.

"Do you know who would want to kill her?" I asked.

Francois stared at me a moment, then set down his cup and saucer. "*I* wanted to kill her yesterday. We have steps in place to assure the right meal goes to the right wedding, and they weren't followed."

"Who's George?" I asked. "I remember her saying that George gave her the keys to the van and told her where to deliver it."

"Yes. George is another employee of mine. I don't like to speak ill of others, but he isn't the brightest bulb in the box and I've told Kara she needs to double-check everything he does and says."

I nodded, wishing I had a notebook. Why would he keep George on if the man didn't meet his expectations? "What about Kara's personal life? Was she married? Kids?"

"No. She had a horrible boyfriend I've been telling her to leave for months. A real jerk. She had come to work a couple of times with some bruises and when I asked her about them, she always said something like she banged her head into a cupboard."

"So you think the boyfriend hurt her?"

"I do."

"That's a shame," Mama murmured.

"It truly was," Francois said.

"Do you think he could have killed her?" I asked.

"I don't know," Francois replied. "Everything was so chaotic yesterday, I suppose he could have approached her without anyone noticing. She did mention they had a fight the previous night and she was going to leave him. Whether she actually ever told him that or not, I'm not sure."

Interesting. Perhaps Kara's untimely death was triggered by domestic violence.

"What's his name?" I asked.

"Bobby Ness. He goes by Bubba. He and Kara lived together. If you want to talk to him, I can give you her address."

"I would very much like to pay my respects," I said, ignoring Mama's glare. She didn't want me near anyone who laid hands on women, and Derek would take issue with it as well. "Did you hear from the Italian family?"

Francois sighed and rubbed his temples. "Oh, yes. Mr. Russo phoned me yesterday afternoon while you and I discovered the noodles. The call went to voicemail, but I did speak to him later as I rushed over there to try to smooth things over. Kara was supposed to follow me, but we all know what happened."

"What did Mr. Russo have to say?" Mama asked.

"He said in his former life, I would be six feet under right now," Francois replied. "Thank goodness he's in witness protection and can't follow through without severe consequences."

"You better watch yourself just in case," Mama warned him. "You've seen those Italian mob shows. They show no mercy."

"Yes, and I ruined his daughter's wedding. I'll be lucky if I ever work in this town again."

"You'll be fine," Mama said. "You have the church behind you and he has to keep a low profile. He can't draw attention to himself if he's in witness protection. It'll all blow over and no one will ever be the wiser. Besides, you've been a catering staple in this area for over a decade. It's not like you're a new person in town who flubbed up and hasn't proven their abilities over and over again."

Mama sounded so sure of herself, but I wouldn't be the least bit surprised if Francois was "disappeared," as they say in those mob shows she mentioned.

"Thank you, Jennifer," he said, reaching across the coffee table and taking her hand. "My company has never made such a horrible faux pas as we did yesterday. Our reputation has always been stellar."

As Mama tried to bolster Francois' self-confidence to pre-wedding levels, I thought about the mob family. I'd never consider killing someone because of a mistake on my wedding, but I hadn't been involved with the mob, either.

Francois had given me two interesting suspects to consider. First, Kara's boyfriend. Had they fought and he became so enraged, he killed her? But why at the wedding? Why not at home? Because he'd be the only suspect then. Doing it at a wedding offered him cover and a lot of potential killers for the police to examine.

Then, the mob family—the Russos. I'd have to think about them and if I decided to follow up, I'd have to think of a way to find them. If Mama didn't like me talking to a potential abuser, she sure wouldn't be comfortable with me dropping in on a former mob enforcer.

And Francois... I'd seen him screaming at Kara, his face red, his eyes bugged out. In fact, I'd wondered if he had been about to drop dead of a heart attack he was so mortified at the mix up. I'd never mention it to Mama, but I couldn't help but consider if Francois had killed Kara in a fit of rage. I'd have to ask Derek about the timing. Had he seen Francois leave, or had he come upstairs before he departed?

As for Sheriff Brewer... I'd talked to one person and had three other suspects besides me and my family. Was being an idiot part of the job description of sheriff all across the country? I thought Oak Peak was the only town suffering with stupid law enforcement that couldn't find a finger sticking in their collective eye.

My phone buzzed in my pocket and I excused myself outside when I saw Derek was calling.

"Hey," I said. "What's going on?"

"The company is here to pick up the tables, chairs, and sound system," Derek said. "I'm wrapping up the cords for them right now, and one of them has been cut."

I narrowed my gaze on Mama's car. "Someone cut the cord on the speaker?"

"Exactly. I'm sending you some pictures so you can see yourself."

"That's... that's so strange."

"It's sabotage, Tilly."

"Do you think someone intentionally tried to ruin our wedding?"

"Based on this evidence, I sure do."

Who in the world would want to ruin my wedding?

That was the question I tossed over and over in my mind for the rest of the day. Derek and I didn't get a chance to discuss theories because my parents were always present, but I could tell he was asking himself the same thing. Usually, he was very engaged with those around him, but his eyes glazed over a couple of times and I caught him staring off into the distance once or twice.

Debbie showed up close to dinner time, a bright smile on her face. She practically shouted while telling us how the bakery owner wanted to carry her sugar free line in not just one, but three, stores throughout Louisiana.

"She says she serves those fancy-pants rich people over on Lake Pontchartrain. According to Margarite, they're always watching their calories and their waistlines. She said my line is going to be an easy sell and a sure-fire winner." Debbie raised her hands above her head and shut her eyes, then yelled, "World domination, here I come! I'm the sugar-free sorceress!"

Mama and Hank stared at her bug-eyed as she continued, but Derek and I sat back and smiled. We'd both been on the receiving end of her exuberant outbursts before.

"Oh, my gosh," she said moments later as she fell into a chair. "I'm exhausted."

"That's wonderful, Debbie," I said. "Did you tell Carla yet?"

"I called her on my way back here. She was as excited as me. Who would've thought my product would be in as many as three bakeries in Louisiana?"

Who would have, indeed? With a grin, I hugged my friend, truly happy for her success. She and Carla made such a great team. Apparently, Edna the Psychic's predictions were coming true.

"I think it's time for us to head to bed," Mama said, standing and sending a wink in Hank's direction. "It's getting late for us old folks. You kids keep quiet down here so we can sleep."

"Yeah, you young'uns keep it down," Hank said with a grin. "Don't party too late."

Considering all of us were either in our forties or just a couple years away, I didn't see us lasting past midnight.

When I heard my parents' door shut, I motioned for both Debbie and Derek to follow me out back.

"Is Irwin out here?" Debbie asked. "I'm wearing leather shoes."

"What does that have to do with anything?" Derek whispered.

"Is he going to be upset with me about that? That I'm wearing one of his fellow animals? Or is he going to want to snack on me when he smells them? Do gators like leather?"

"Irwin couldn't care less about your shoes. Follow me," I said, my voice hushed.

We walked about twenty yards away from the house toward the water, the only light being from the full moon. The humid air almost seemed suffocating, as did the mosquitoes.

"Listen!" I hissed as Debbie began to complain. "We have a problem!"

"Another one besides the murder?"

"Yes. Derek said that someone cut the wire to the speaker. That's why the music never played during the ceremony."

Debbie's brow furrowed as she slapped her arms trying to ward off the onslaught of blood suckers. "Seriously? So someone was intentionally messing with the wedding?"

"That's what it looked like to me," Derek said. "That wire was sliced clean through. Cut. It wasn't frayed."

"Was there a test done beforehand to make sure it was working?" Debbie asked. "Before I got here? Maybe the company provided a faulty speaker?"

"I ran a test the night before the ceremony," Derek replied, and we all exchanged glances while trying to come up with some other logical scenario for the sliced wire.

"Well, someone wanting to mess with the wedding is one thing, but murdering another person takes things to a whole other playing field," Debbie said. "Do you honestly think they're related? That someone would go to that extent to screw up a wedding?"

"I don't know," I said with a shrug. "That's what we're discussing."

"And let's not forget about Irwin," Derek said. "That gator didn't show up for two days. Hank said he'd fed him before we arrived and he thought he'd stay down by the water. Then he strolls up in the middle of the ceremony? What are the chances of that?"

"Well, I'm not overly-educated on alligator behavior, so I don't have any insider information," Debbie replied.

Both stared at me for an answer. I recalled my childhood and teenage years. Irwin came and went at will without any sort of schedule, but I did find it odd he showed up at the most inopportune time imaginable on my wedding day.

A light breeze wafted through the night and felt wonderfully cooling over my skin. However, it also brought the distinct odor of rotting fish with it.

"Oh, man. That's awful," Debbie said with a grimace as she covered her nose. "Where's that coming from?"

I turned toward the water. In my experience, most people didn't clean their fish outside because the odor attracted gators. The stench definitely smelled like a lot of fish guts had been left to rot.

After pulling out my phone, I turned on the flashlight. "Let's go find what's causing it."

"I don't need to go trotting down to the water at night to know the smell is rotting fish," Debbie said.

Ignoring her, I raised my phone and began walking. Derek followed, and after whispering a few curses, so did Debbie.

The waterline shone brightly in the moonlight through the trees, and the gentle lapping of the water against the shore sounded in the distance. I covered my nose and mouth as we ventured farther away from the house.

"Aim it over there," Derek instructed. "By that tree. Something is lying there."

The light caught something shiny, about a foot long. The stench grew stronger as we approached.

"That's one big fish," Debbie said as we stared at the dead creature. "Do you know what kind it is, Tilly?

I shook my head. "Maybe a bass? I never was a big fishing person."

"Would Hank know?" Derek asked.

"Yes. He can identify anything that lives in the water."

"Why is this fully intact rotting fish sitting up here on land away from the water?" Debbie mused.

"Great question," Derek murmured as I glanced

back at the house. The porch light had been turned on. "I don't think the fish got here all by itself."

"Let's head back," I said. "I think we woke my parents."

As I tossed around why a full fish would be found on the lawn, an answer began to form.

"Who's there?" Hank called out, the sound of a shotgun being cocked ringing in the air. "Identify yourself by the count of three, or I'm sending you to your maker."

Debbie gasped and Derek stilled. "It's us, Hank!" I yelled, holding up my illuminated phone. "Tilly, Derek, and Debbie."

"What are you three doing out here?" he said, bringing the shotgun to his side as he strode toward us, and I noted he'd thankfully put on some sweatpants. It wouldn't be the first time I'd seen him running around out back in only his boxers and cowboy boots. "I thought y'all had gone to bed."

"We were wondering why Irwin showed up at the wedding when he did," Debbie explained.

"He lives here. This is his house," Hank said. "We share this land with him. That's why he decided to attend."

"I don't know," I said. "Can you follow us?"

"What for?"

"I want to show you something."

"Okay, honey. Lead the way."

We traipsed back across the yard to the tree and I shined my light on the fish.

"What the heck?" Hank whispered as he bent over to inspect the corpse. "That's a bass. What's it doing on my lawn?"

"I'm wondering if it was left here," I said. "Maybe to lure Irwin in."

"But why wouldn't he eat it?" Debbie asked.

"I don't know," Hank muttered, standing. "Let's head down to the water."

As we followed him, I felt a lot better about being out so late at night, especially with Hank carrying a gun. I knew the wilds of Louisiana could be dangerous with not only gators, but snakes and snapping turtles.

"Shine that light along the edge, honey," Hank murmured.

We slowly walked along the water, and despite the heat, a chill of fear raced over my skin. The nocturnal animals called to each other while the mosquitoes buzzed around us, yet it seemed quieter than death.

"Well, well, well," Hank said. "Looky there."

A fish head lay on the grass, as well as a tail.

"What does it mean?" Debbie asked.

"First and foremost, someone caught some fish and let them go to waste, which gets my boxers in a big knot," Hank said. "Based on the bite marks, Irwin had quite a feast."

He turned back toward the house and began walking. We found more fish parts along the way until we reached the intact carcass.

"This is where he got full, I'm guessing," Hank said. "Then he decided to come up and say hello."

"So you think the fish were placed there intentionally?" I asked.

"I most certainly do. I didn't leave them lying around, and last time I checked, fish needed water to live."

"How do you know it was Irwin who ate them?" Derek asked. "Couldn't it have been another gator?"

"No, not a chance, son," Hank replied. "Gators are territorial. This is Irwin's slice of land. I've seen him go around with another male who wanted to move in. It was a battle, but Irwin chased him off. No one wants to tangle with my boy."

Hank stopped and glanced around for a moment when we got closer to the house and a sound came from the side area, where Kara had been killed. "Can you shine your phone around again, honey? I'd hate to disturb Irwin while he's resting. He can be a bit cranky if he doesn't get his sleep."

We found him under a different tree than this afternoon. Hank gave him a wide birth as we returned the last few yards to the house.

"Let's get inside before the bugs make mincemeat out of us," Debbie said.

We filed into the living room, plopping down on the couches with a collective sigh.

"Hank, if those fish were used to lure Irwin up to the house, how was that done?" I asked. "The timing was perfect for him to ruin our wedding."

"Like I said when you arrived, I hadn't seen Irwin in a few days, but that didn't mean the boy wasn't lurking around. Gators are territorial, so he couldn't have just been feeling a little salty and decided to hang out in the water. But throw an easy meal at him, and he'll jump on that. Overall, gators are lazy and will always go for the simplest buffet presented."

I imagined someone moving through the trees on my wedding day placing fish around until they arrived at the water. With Francois and Kara here, as well as the guests arriving, they could have easily gone unnoticed. It was definitely feasible.

Debbie stood and stretched her arms over her head, then wiped away a bead of sweat from her brow. "I'm heading to bed," she said. "It's late and I'm hotter than Satan's undies. I need to sit in front of that fan for a bit."

We said goodnight as she ascended the stairs.

Derek grabbed my hand and gave it a squeeze. "We know for sure that the speaker wire was cut, and now we can assume that the fish were planted in order to lure Irwin up to the wedding."

Hank nodded and yawned. "I think that's a fair thing to say. Those fish didn't flop up onto land by themselves."

Someone had gone to great pains to ruin my wedding.

But was it the same person who killed Kara? I would believe so until I could prove otherwise.

CHAPTER 7

*I*n the early morning hours, it occurred to me that perhaps all this chaos *wasn't* about me or our wedding day. Perhaps it had to do with ruining something else... or in this case, someone.

Derek and Hank left to go on a boat ride, Mama said she had work to do at the church, and Debbie was on the phone with Carla about financial stuff. I slipped out and drove our rental car to Francois'. I definitely did my best sleuthing when I didn't have someone around who cared about me and kept telling me to be careful.

"My goodness, Tilly," he said as he answered. "What a surprise this is! I wasn't expecting you!"

He'd pulled himself together since the last time

I'd seen him and looked rested. His mustache still seemed crooked to me, and I'd given up trying to decide if it was fake or not.

"I was wondering if I could get the number for the Italian bride," I said. "I had a couple of questions for her."

"About what?" Francois asked.

Dang it. I hated when I had to lie. "I'm thinking about having another ceremony, and I wanted to know who she used besides you. Who did her chairs? The sound system? Things like that. We weren't happy with the last company."

"Come in, come in," Francois said as I followed him into the kitchen. "When are you thinking of having the other ceremony?"

"I'm not sure if we'll even do it," I said noncommittally as I glanced around. Did he ever prepare food and eat in this kitchen? Not even a breadcrumb could be found. "Just gathering some ideas for now."

Francois jotted down a number and an address. "She's horrible about answering her phone, and I know she's supposed to leave for her honeymoon either today or tomorrow. I can't remember which."

"Thanks," I replied, taking the slip of paper and shoving it in my jeans pocket.

"I hope if you do decide to have another wedding,

you'll allow me to redeem myself," Francois said with a smile.

"Of course," I replied. "I know you're the best. If we move forward, we'll definitely include you in our plans."

We chatted for a few more minutes, then I took my leave. Once in the car, I dialed Nicola, the Italian bride, but as Francois had predicted, it went straight to voicemail.

"I'm coming to see you, my new friend," I muttered as I entered her address into my phone.

Normally, I wasn't one to arrive at anybody's home unannounced, especially someone I'd never met. However, if Nicola was taking off for her honeymoon and I had the heavy umbrella of me or my loved ones potentially being charged with murder hanging over me, I'd traipse in unexpectedly without hesitation.

Fifteen minutes later, I drove by a small marina filled with boats, and arrived at the address—an upscale apartment building. As I walked through the grassy grounds accented with flowering azalea bushes, I passed a man dragging two suitcases. I smiled, hoping I looked like I had business at the complex besides blindsiding a bride.

I found the apartment door wide open and knocked.

A woman in her twenties came around the corner wearing a yellow sundress, her black hair piled up in a bun. "Yes?"

"Nicola?"

"Who wants to know?" she asked, crossing her arms over her chest and narrowing her gaze.

"I'm Tilly Bordeaux. We were married on the same day. Well, I was supposed to be married but that was put on the back burner when an alligator showed up and a woman was murdered."

"Oh, my gosh! The Creole food girl!"

"Yes."

"How can you eat that stuff?"

"It's an acquired taste."

"Come in, come in," she said, motioning me into the living room. I sat on the black leather sofa and glanced around. Nice place. Crisp. Clean. Modern. Not my style in the least bit—I preferred cozy and comfortable—but to each their own.

"What's up?" she asked, settling in a chair across from me.

"I was wondering if you ever got married, or if your wedding was ruined by the wrong food."

"Oh, we got married," she said. "After the cere-mony, my father lost his temper when he saw what the caterer had brought. Everyone left, but we were officially married."

"Oh, wow."

"You said an alligator showed up at your house?" she asked.

"Yes. We had an outside wedding by the water, and an alligator strolled in during the vows and sent everyone scrambling."

I didn't bother to explain the gator happened to be my stepfather's pet—that would lead to a lot of questions I didn't have time to answer.

"So, you still aren't married?"

I shook my head. "No."

"That's a real shame," Nicola said. "What a horrible thing to happen."

"Yes. That, topped with the noodles instead of the Creole food... it made for a mess of a day. Of course, one of Francois' employees was killed, which was awful."

"I heard someone died at your wedding. How terribly sad for them, and scary for you."

"It was," I said, nodding. "I feel awful for Kara, the woman who was murdered."

"Are you sure she didn't keel over in a heart

attack or something?" Nicola asked. "Or did the police confirm she was killed?"

The man I'd seen dragging the two suitcases behind him entered empty-handed. He smiled, gave me a quick wave, then went down the hall.

"Well, I found her with a knife in her chest," I replied. "I can say without a doubt, and without police clarification, that it was murder."

Nicola's eyes widened as she brought her hand to her mouth. "How awful. Do they know who did it?"

"That's why I'm here. I was wondering if you thought your dad had anything to do with it." She narrowed her gaze on me, and I realized I should have been a little more tactful. "I heard he used to work for some unsavory characters and he's in federal protection and he was terribly upset about the food mix up. I was thinking perhaps he had the caterer killed for revenge or something? For messing up the meal?"

"Wow," she said shaking her head. "You come in here and accuse my father of murder?"

Yeah, I probably should have tip-toed around that with a little more finesse, but the pressure of discovering the killer before the sheriff hauled my loved ones off to jail weighed heavily upon me.

"I'm sorry," I said. "I want to find out who's

responsible for ruining my wedding and who took the life of that poor woman."

"Shouldn't the police be worrying about solving the murder?"

"Well, they are, but..." I had no idea how to finish my sentence. How did I explain that one of my family members may go to prison for a crime they didn't commit?

"The old gossip tree is alive and well, I see," Nicola muttered. "I don't understand how my father is supposed to stay hidden if people keep talking about him."

"Trust me, it's like that everywhere," I said with a shrug, firmly convinced that people sticking their nose in others' business boiled down to human nature.

Nicola sighed and stared out the sliding glass door for a few very uncomfortable minutes while she gathered her thoughts. "My father has an... interesting past," she said. "I was young, and I don't know much about it. I've heard bits and pieces, but we pretend it never happened. Our lives are here now, and we focus on that."

The man emerged from the hallway with two more suitcases and headed out the door.

"That's my new husband," Nicola said softly, her eyes shining with happiness. "Isn't he cute?"

I hadn't noticed, but I nodded and smiled.

"He's an absolute darling," Nicola continued. "I love him to bits. I'm so lucky."

Nicola wanted to make puppy eyes at her new husband, and I needed to find a killer. Back to the conversation. "Do you know anyone who would want to hurt Francois' business?"

"Oh, heck yes," she said, pulling on the band that held her hair in the bun. The black waves cascaded around her shoulders and she quickly gathered them up again. "My wedding was a big deal in this area. I'm not bragging, just stating facts."

"Of course."

"Every florist and caterer wanted me to use them. They all know about my dad... it's like the worst kept secret ever. They all would have loved to say they serviced his daughter's wedding, so they fawned over me and tried to get my business. The new caterer in the area was particularly aggressive... Cathy's Catering."

Interesting.

"Really? How so?"

"She promised me she would meet Francois' pricing and said some horrible things about him."

"Like what?"

"Oh, my gosh... well, things like she'd heard of a whole wedding party getting sick from food he'd prepared. That he overcharged. He did a vegan wedding and didn't tell the bride he'd used sardines in the salad dressing. Things like that."

"Apparently, you didn't believe her," I ventured.

"No. I asked around and decided she was lying. After a while, she seemed desperate and her stories became ridiculous."

Desperate people did desperate things, and maybe Cathy from Cathy's Catering was frustrated with Francois' impeccable reputation and his long-time success in the area. Could she have killed Kara to damage Francois?

It was certainly possible.

I smiled and cleared my throat. "Do you know of anyone else who would want to hurt Francois' reputation?"

Nicola pursed her lips for a moment, then shook her head. "No, I don't. Only Cathy's Catering. The wedding business is pretty cutthroat."

"Yes, I agree," I replied, feeling as though this conversation had ended—at least on my side. "Thanks so much for talking to me, Nicola. I appreciate your time."

"I do hope you find the time to say your vows," she said, standing. "It's wonderful to marry the person you love. It binds you forever."

We said our goodbyes, and I weaved my way down the pathway toward my rental car. The visit hadn't been a total loss. Cathy's Catering had jumped to the top of my list of suspects. Francois had been in the area for a long time, and it would be difficult to dethrone him as catering king—but having two weddings mistakes and one of his employees dead all in the same day would be a good start.

Nicola's husband loaded the suitcases into a car two parking spaces down from mine. He smiled and waved as I approached.

"Hey," he said, walking over to me. "I heard you in there talking to Nicola."

"Yes. I didn't catch your name before."

"I'm Mark Setzer. Nicola's horrible about introducing me to new people. Sorry about that."

"It's nice to meet you," I said as we shook hands. "I'm Tilly. Congratulations on your marriage."

"Thanks."

He glanced over his shoulder, then turned back to me. "You're the Creole food girl, right?"

Apparently, my dining choices had made quite the impression. "That's me."

"I heard you ask if you thought Nicola's father could have had anything to do with the murder at your wedding."

"I did," I said as my cheeks heated. I'd offended the bride, and now apparently the groom as well. Sometimes, if I wasn't falling over air, I tripped over my tongue. "I'm sorry about that. It's just that—"

"Listen to me," he hissed, stepping forward. My heart thundered as fear washed through me. Was he going to throw a punch? "Nicola's father is a mean bastard. Yes, he was in the mob. No, I don't know what he did for the organization. He was *furious* about the food. So mad, I thought maybe he would have a heart attack."

"Oh, my word. That's not good. I'm sorry he became so upset!"

"Here's the thing, Tilly. I tried to break up with Nicola three months ago. I found out she was cheating on me, and I didn't want any part of it. Her father *broke into my apartment* one night while I was sleeping and told me that if I didn't marry his daughter, there'd be consequences."

I gasped and brought my hand to my mouth. "Like what?"

"He said he'd take me out to the Gulf of Mexico,

chain my feet to a cement block, and throw me over-board. If he broke into my apartment and threatened me like that, ask yourself if he's capable of killing over a bunch of noodles. The answer is yes. One hundred percent."

"Are you pulling my leg?" I asked, horrified by what Mark claimed. Was it some type of prank? It sounded like something right out of the movies!

"I wish I was," he whispered, glancing over his shoulder again. "I feel like I'm being watched all the time."

"What are you going to do? Have you called the police?"

I immediately regretted my question. The cops were proving themselves to be just as dumb as the ones in Oak Peak. They probably wouldn't believe his story.

"No. They're on Russo's payroll," Mark said.

"They won't help me. They'd probably be the ones to dump me overboard."

We stared at each other a beat as I digested his predicament. "What are you going to do?"

"I don't know," he replied, running his hand through his hair. "I can't do this, though. I can't stay married to Nicola. Even last night I heard her on the phone with her boyfriend. He's going to meet us in the Caribbean. Can you believe that?"

"Why did she marry you if she wants to be with someone else?" I asked.

"She's like her father. People are not people—they're possessions. She wanted me, but she wants other people as well. I have to disappear for my own sanity."

I imagined Mark on the run living off fish he caught and coconuts he picked from the trees in the Caribbean while looking over his shoulder the rest of his life.

"If there's any way I can help you, please call me," I said, pulling one of my business cards from my bag. "I'm not sure what I can do, but please know someone is rooting for you."

He glanced down at the card and his face paled. "You're a reporter?"

"Yes. But not anywhere in Louisiana. Oak Peak is

in California. My parents live here, so we decided to get married at their home."

"I see," he said, his shoulders relaxing. "I better get back to Nicola or she'll call her father on me."

"Good luck."

As I drove away, I took a few deep breaths. My list of suspects kept getting longer and a few kept vying for top spot. Between Mr. Russo being upset about his daughter's wedding and Cathy's Catering trying to edge in on Francois' business, both were definitely contenders for not only wanting to ruin my wedding, but to get revenge on Francois.

I ARRIVED AT MY PARENTS' house to find Debbie sitting outside talking to Irwin, who was lying in the sun about twenty feet away. They faced each other, and I wondered what Irwin thought of the new girl who had invaded his space. I didn't want to scare Debbie, but she probably shouldn't be alone with the beast.

"Where did you go?" she asked. "I got off the phone a few minutes ago and realized you weren't around."

"I went to visit the noodle bride," I said, settling into the lawn chair next to her.

"Why did you do that?"

"I wanted to see if her father could have been so upset about the food mix up, he decided to get revenge on Francois for it."

"Interesting. And what did you find out?"

"It's definitely a possibility." I explained that Russo had been furious, was a former member of the mob in protective custody, and Mark's situation with Nicola.

"Unbelievable," Debbie muttered as she shut her eyes. "People are crazy everywhere, not just in Oak Peak."

"You got that right. I wish I knew what to do to help poor Mark. It seems he doesn't have a choice on what to do with his life."

"He doesn't," Debbie replied. "Did you tell him to go to the police?"

"Yes," I said with a sigh. "He says they're on Russo's payroll."

We sat in silence for a few moments and I wondered if Debbie had drifted off to sleep. A nice cloud cover and moved in along with a slight breeze, and it actually made me a little tired as well. If I didn't have an alligator staring me down, perhaps I'd doze off, too.

"Do you believe him?" Debbie asked, her voice groggy.

"Believe what?"

"That the police are on Russo's payroll?"

"I don't have any reason not to," I replied with a shrug. "Mark seemed upset and desperate."

"If that's the case, they may be the ones who are responsible for the murder."

"How do you figure that?" I asked, turning on my side to face her.

Debbie opened her eyes. "Russo gets upset at Francois about the noodles. He calls the cops and tells them to make Francois pay. They kill Kara."

"But there weren't any cops here until after the body was found," I said.

"Maybe they were in plainclothes," Debbie replied with a shrug. "Things got pretty crazy after Irwin sauntered in. We may not have noticed who should be on the property and who shouldn't."

Debbie had a valid point, which worried me. If the people responsible for the murder were the ones investigating it, that was like having a drug addict keep an eye on the heroin.

"Do you think that could be what happened?" I asked.

"I don't see why not, Tilly. You've been investigating a lot of murders, and we've seen some wild stuff. Crazy isn't limited to Oak Peak."

"You're right."

Glancing over my shoulder, I found Hank and Derek strolling out, Hank carrying a bag of marshmallows.

"Hey, lovely ladies!" he called. "What are you two up to today?"

"Hey, Hank!" Debbie yelled, coming alive once again. "We're discussing the mob and the police."

"Oh, my," Hank said with a chuckle. "Let me spend some time with Irwin and then I'll join you and you can tell me all about it."

Derek pulled up a chair next to mine and sat down.

"How was your boat ride?"

"Amazing," he said, shaking his head. "We saw so much wildlife and he told a few stories... I love spending time with your dad. He's different from anyone I've ever met."

I smiled and squeezed his hand. Derek was right —Hank was one of a kind. "I'm glad you had fun. I need to have him take me out with him one day, as well. It's been a long time since I've been deep in the swamps."

"It's creepy as heck in there, but also beautiful," Derek said. "And also kind of... I'm at a loss for the right word. Perhaps mystical?"

"I agree. It's like if you did actually see a ghost walking across the water, you wouldn't be all that surprised."

"Yes! Exactly."

"I want to go on the boat with Hank as well," Debbie said. "We can forget about crooked cops and murderers for a bit and have him take us, Tilly."

"Great idea," I replied.

"Crooked cops?" Derek asked, glancing over at me with worry in his gaze. "I don't think I like the sound of that."

"We'll tell you about it when Hank finishes up," I said.

Hank stood about five feet in front of Irwin holding a marshmallow between two fingertips. Irwin opened his huge jaws and Hank tossed it in. They continued the practice for a few more minutes, then Hank walked over and patted Irwin on the back. "You're my good boy," he said. "Do you want your bath?"

Debbie and Derek exchanged confused glances.

"Derek, can you give me a hand, son?" Hank asked. Derek shot to his feet and followed the older man into the garage.

Something caught my gaze by the side fence. I could have sworn I caught sight of a ghostly image resembling Kara, but it faded faster than it registered. After staring at the spot for a few seconds, I decided I was losing my mind.

Moments later, the two men returned with a large green plastic tub measuring about ten feet long. "I cleaned up Irwin's bath for the wedding," Hank said. "But it's hot out and I'm sure he misses his bath time."

As Hank filled the container with water from the hose, he sent Derek back into the garage to fetch a box. He emerged a few moments later, just as the tub was brimming.

"Okay, Irwin!" Hank said. "Get on over here! We've got your duckies as well!"

Debbie burst out into peals of laughter as the gator hurried over and climbed into the tub. Derek stepped back, rightfully leery of the beast, and handed the box to Hank, who pulled out six yellow rubber ducks and dumped them in the water. Irwin grabbed one in his huge jaws and began rolling.

"Amazing," Debbie said, wiping her eyes. "I can't believe this is your dad's life."

It definitely wouldn't be considered normal, but it's how I'd grown up. Hank had always insisted that everyone keep their distance from Irwin, except him. "He says he and Irwin share a special bond," I said. "It is definitely interesting."

"That's putting it mildly," Derek said as he sat down again.

A moment later, Hank pulled up a chair and lowered himself into it with a sigh. "Now, tell me about the mob, Tilly. Sounds like some juicy stuff."

Everyone listened intently as I recounted my conversation with Nicola. When I finished, Hank stroked his beard and Derek groaned.

"That boy, Mark, has gotten himself in a bit of a pickle," Hank murmured.

"Messing with the mob isn't something we need to be doing," Derek said.

"Oh, I agree." Hank nodded. "But this possible police involvement bothers me. Sheriff Marvin Brewer has always been a bit slimy, but I always thought all politicians were. Perhaps his slipperiness runs deeper than I thought."

"If Russo told the cops to help him get his revenge on Francois and they ended up killing Kara, it doesn't bode well for us that they are investigating the murder," Debbie said.

"Brewer did say he thought one of us did it," I said. "No one would expect a cop to actually be a killer and we'd be easy targets, especially since things got so crazy so fast."

Debbie sighed. "Very true. Irwin really messed everything up, but we think that may have been intentional, right?"

"Yes," I replied. "Someone led him up from the water with the fish."

"Amazing timing on that one. Y'all follow me over to the side of the house," Hank said. "Let's walk through this real quick."

We all trailed behind him, giving Irwin a wide berth, and again, I thought I saw Kara's ghost. Glancing over at Hank, I noted he was also staring at the same spot, his face contorted in confusion.

"So, Derek and I were right here," Hank said, his gaze now focused on Derek. "All those darn noodles were over there." He shook his head and placed his hands on his hips. "I'm still in mourning we didn't get our meal."

"We all are," Debbie said. "I was looking forward to trying real Creole cuisine for the first time."

"Very sad day on so many levels," Hank said,

turning to me. "Tilly, you were here for a while, then you went upstairs to change, right?"

"Yes," I replied.

"Debbie, you hung out here for a bit after Tilly left."

"Yes. I went inside shortly after her."

"Tilly, your mama was here, too," Hank said. "She was crying, and that really set me off. I don't like seeing my wife crying."

"I was furious as well," Derek replied. "I had a hunch Tilly was upset and she just wasn't showing it."

He knew me so well.

"Yeah, I recall that," Hank said, nodding. "You and I both had some choice words for Francois and Kara."

"We did," Derek agreed. "I feel bad about it now, especially that Kara's dead."

"Did you two mention that to Sheriff Brewer when he took our statements?" I asked.

"I did," Hank said. "I probably shouldn't have, now that he mentioned he's looking at one of us as the murderer."

"What happened next?" I asked.

"Well, the rain started coming down," Hank said. "Kara and Francois were scrambling to get everything packed up. Your mama went inside, and Derek and I helped them out a bit, then Francois left."

"If you were so mad, why did you help them?" I asked.

Hank shrugged and stroked his beard. "I'd said my piece. The poor girl was in tears. Francois looked like his boxers were in a bunch, and I thought I'd put everything aside and help everyone get where they wanted to go."

"I went upstairs to find you," Derek said.

"Did you ever notice anyone by the van?" I asked.

"No, I did not," Hank said. "The van was parked over there, the back end halfway through the gate so Francois and Kara could easily set up the serving tables and bring in the food."

"You couldn't see anyone out front. Is that right?"

"Yes, honey. But we could hear them all leaving after Irwin showed up."

I walked over to the gate and opened it wide, then stepped through while recalling the slamming car doors and voices of my wedding guests as they'd dispersed.

The space was just big enough for the van and someone to scoot back and forth along the side of the vehicle to reach the doors, which was exactly the way I remembered it: hurrying over to the van and moving past the fence to find Kara in the driver's seat.

I rubbed my temples as a headache formed behind my eyes. A theory on who the sheriff was targeting began to form.

Even though anyone could have struck from the front of the house, Brewer had stated he thought someone in my family had been the killer.

Could he have Hank in his crosshairs?

My stepdad had stolen the girl—my mom—many years ago, and now Brewer would get his revenge and make Hank look as guilty as possible.

Hank had been the last one in my family to see Kara alive, and I'd found her. The sheriff didn't want to arrest me, which would only hurt my mom, the one he most likely still loved. That only left Hank, and with him out of the picture, Brewer had a direct path to Mama.

It was the perfect set up.

At first sunlight, I found Debbie downstairs.

"So what do we need to do to get this murder wrapped up?" Debbie asked while we enjoyed a cup of coffee. "I've got ants in my pants. I need to get home and help Carla."

"Tell the sheriff you need to head back to Oak Peak to run your business," I said. "You aren't the one he's after."

"I'm not? How do you know?"

"Because I think he wants to pin it on Hank," I replied, sipping my coffee.

"Well, that's not right."

"No, it isn't. I need to fix it."

Debbie sighed and added more cream to her

mug. "Then back to my original question: what do we need to do to find the killer?"

"I'm not really sure."

And I wasn't. I still couldn't figure out if the person who ruined my wedding and the one who killed Kara were one and the same. Or were there two different entities at work? But why? How?

"There are a couple of different reasons why I can see that someone would want Kara dead," I said, hoping that if I talked it out, a bright spotlight would suddenly shine down on the correct answer. "First, she had a nasty boyfriend. Francois said he hit her and she was breaking up with him, but Francois wasn't sure if she'd let the boyfriend know. If she had, he could have killed her."

"A crime of passion."

"Or rage—whatever you want to call it."

"Go on," Debbie urged.

"Then the Russos were furious they didn't get their noodles, and Mr. Russo has a horrible history with the mob. I don't think old habits die that hard for some people. He could have killed Kara in revenge for his daughter's wedding being messed up."

"Very true. Once a mob guy, always a mob guy."

"You don't know that for sure," I said.

"I know, but it sounded good. Keep going with your theories."

I laughed and tried to find my train of thought. "Of course, Cathy's Catering wants Francois' business, so she could be trying to ruin his reputation, and what better way to do that than to have two weddings go awry, one with a dead woman?"

"But that doesn't answer the problem with the speaker wire or the fish leading Irwin up from the water," Debbie countered.

"I know. I'm wondering if we're dealing with two separate issues. Someone who wanted to mess with my wedding and someone who had a problem with Kara."

Debbie stared at me a beat with a furrowed brow before speaking. "Why in the world would you think that?"

"Because nothing else makes sense!" I said, throwing my hands up in the air. "Who in the world would want my wedding ruined and someone dead all in one horrible afternoon?"

She pinched her lips together and glanced around the kitchen as if searching for an answer. "Good point. That would be going to extreme measures. Do you think the death and everything that happened during the wedding was coincidence?"

"Yes. Except the rain. No one can control the sky."

"So what's on the agenda today?"

I glanced over my shoulder into the living room to make sure no one listened in on the conversation. "I want to go visit Kara's boyfriend."

"The abuser?"

"Yes. And I want you to go with me."

"Of course."

Debbie didn't even blink before agreeing. I grinned at my friend, appreciating her more than ever. "We can't let my parents and Derek know, though."

"No, we can't. The hissy fit would be epic and well-deserved. If you want to do stupid things, you come to me first."

We both burst out laughing as Derek walked in. "What's so funny?"

"I read that Oak Peak got a spring snowstorm," Debbie said without missing a beat. "We were laughing at their misery."

"Well, we do need the water," Derek said, filling his mug.

"Oh, yes, we do. I'm just glad I'm not there for it," Debbie replied, giving me a wink.

"What are you two up to today?" Derek asked as he sat down. "Anything fun and exciting?"

"Tilly and I are going to visit a couple of other bakeries and see if they'll carry my goods," Debbie said.

I dreaded lying to Derek, and Debbie apparently knew it. The falsehood flowed from her with such ease, I squirmed in my seat as guilt washed over me.

"Sounds like something I should skip," Derek said, smiling.

"Probably," Debbie replied. "Us bakers are a chatty bunch. Who knows how long we'll be gone?"

Mama and Hank hurried into the kitchen for their second and third cups of brew, and both announced they'd be leaving for the day.

"My buddy needs some help with his boat," Hank said. "Something's wrong with the engine. You're welcome to tag along if you like, Derek."

"That would be great. Thanks."

"I've got some things to do at the church again," Mama said. "I'll be gone a few hours at the most."

"We should head out to dinner and get some Creole food this evening," Hank suggested. "I've been dreaming about crawfish and jambalaya."

"That sounds like a great idea," Mama agreed.

It did sound delicious, but it only reminded me that Derek and I still weren't married. Yet, I couldn't bring myself to have even a small ceremony with the possible threat of Hank going to prison for a crime he didn't commit.

The sheriff would be dropping the hammer soon, and time was wasting. I needed to find the killer.

"We better get going, Debbie," I said, standing.

"Yes. You're right," she replied. "Just let me brush my teeth. I don't want to offend any potential buyers with my horrid coffee breath."

As she scampered up the stairs, Derek turned to me. "Can I talk to you a minute in the living room?"

"Sure."

My cheeks heated as I followed him out of the kitchen because I had a feeling about what he was going to say.

"I know you aren't going to talk to bakers," he said, taking my hands in his. "Your cheeks turned the color of apples when Debbie mentioned that, so I think she was lying."

Staring at the floor, I pursed my lips together, suddenly feeling like a small child being chastised.

"Just tell me where you're going and what you're doing," he continued. "I'm not going to stop you, but if I know what your plans are, I'll feel better about it."

"We're going to see Kara's boyfriend," I replied, meeting his gaze. "He goes by Bubba."

"How very southern," Derek said with a chuckle. "Will you please call me when you're done there so I'll know you're safe?"

"Yes," I said, sighing. "I'm sorry. I'm always afraid you're going to tell me what to do and what not to do."

"I won't, unless you plan on doing something really, really stupid. In this case, I'm glad you're taking Debbie," Derek said, then kissed the tip of my nose. "Do you want me to tag along?"

"Do you want to?" I asked, hoping he said no. I loved him, but I didn't want him to be able to stop me from talking with Bubba.

"What I want is for you to be safe. Do you think I should go? Do you feel you'll be in danger?"

"No, I don't," I said. "If I were visiting him alone, that would be one thing. But I have Debbie with me. We'll be fine."

Derek nodded. "I agree. Just be careful, okay?"

"We will."

Debbie came thundering down the stairs. "Ready?"

"Yes, let's go." I turned to the kitchen and yelled, "Bye, Hank! Bye, Mama!"

"Have fun, girls!" Mama called.

Confronting a man who laid his hands on a woman wouldn't be considered fun by any standards. "We will!" I yelled and squeezed Derek's hand.

WHEN WE ARRIVED at the apartment building, I easily found a parking spot. The complex had definitely seen better days. Empty flower beds lined the walkway and paint peeled from the walls. I guessed rent would be a lot cheaper here than at Nicola's place.

"It's this way," Debbie said, pointing to the right. "That's building A, and we need E."

When we arrived at the correct apartment, Debbie tapped on the door. "He better have that air conditioning going full blast or I'm going to be really cranky. I'm so hot, I feel like I may melt."

"I know," I said, wiping a bead of sweat from my cheek. "I can't believe I used to live here and it never bothered me."

"We need our dry mountain air," Debbie muttered. "This humidity is for the birds."

A bald man in his thirties dressed in a white tank top and cut off denim shorts answered.

"Yeah?"

"Bubba?" I asked.

"Who wants to know?"

Interesting. The same response Nicola had given me. Did Bubba have something to hide as Nicola did, or was he just a jerk?

Debbie and I exchanged glances. "Well, my name's Tilly, and this is Debbie. We were friends of Kara's. We wanted to stop by and give our condolences."

"Okay," he said.

"May we come in?" I asked, smiling.

"I guess so. I don't remember Kara talking about no Debbie or Tilly."

The stench of body odor engulfed me as he stepped to the side and I scooted around him. The apartment definitely didn't have the air conditioning running and stank of old beer and unwashed male.

We followed Bubba into the living room, and I noted his limp. The shades had been drawn and beer cans littered the coffee table. A small fan sat on an end table pointed directly at a Barcalounger. Bubba sat down and popped open a beer.

Debbie glanced at the tattered brown sofa, and I

wondered if something would crawl out of it if I were to sit down. Both of us remained standing.

"So, as we were saying, we're very sorry for your loss," Debbie said, her gaze darting around as if she expected something to jump out from the shadows. "I'm sure this must be a hard time for you."

Bubba nodded and took a swig of beer. "Yeah, it is, but Kara told me the morning she was killed that she was leaving me."

"Oh, really?" I asked, feigning surprise. "Why was that?"

"She said she got tired of us always fighting."

"That's a shame," Debbie said. "What were you two arguing about?"

"She was always nagging me. *You need to get a job. I ain't a bank. Please help around the house.* But she knew darn well I'm disabled. Drove me crazy."

He seemed pretty mobile to me. Was he gaming the system? "How did you become disabled?"

"Fishing boat accident," he replied. "Shattered my ankle. Hurts like you can't believe when it rains."

"I'm sorry to hear that," I said. At least that explained the limp. "May I get a glass of water?"

"Sure."

As I walked into the kitchen, it wasn't the sink full of dishes or the line of ants marching across the floor that caught my attention. It was the two cabinets with holes, as if someone had put his fist through them.

I opened a few other cupboards and couldn't find a clean glass. When I turned around, I noted another hole in the wall by the kitchen table.

On the counter sat a calendar. After quickly scanning it, I realized it was Kara's work schedule. My parents' address had been written down on my wedding day.

"So what are you two doing here?" Bubba asked as I returned to the living room. "You want to go through her stuff? See if there's anything to keep?"

"Uh… no," Debbie replied. "We stopped by to say how sorry we are about Kara. That's all."

Bubba sighed and shook his head. "I don't know. Maybe it's a good thing she died. A blessing."

"Excuse me?" I asked, my gaze sliding over to Debbie. "What does that mean?"

"Well, if I couldn't have her, no one should, right? I loved that girl more than anyone. Her leaving and taking up with someone else would have broken my heart. I couldn't live like that."

I couldn't take any more of the oppressive heat or stench, and frankly, Bubba was giving me the creeps. If he couldn't have Kara, no one would? Really?

"We better get going," I said. "I wish you well, Bubba."

Debbie and I hurried out to the car and didn't speak until the air conditioning blasted us in the face. We both sighed in relief.

"I need a shower," Debbie said, leaning her head back against the seat. "That apartment was disgusting. I was afraid to sit down. Something's wrong with that guy."

"Agreed. Do you think he could have killed his girlfriend?"

"Most definitely," Debbie replied. "If he couldn't have her, no one could. He said so himself."

"That's frightening," I said. A chill ran down my spine.

"Yes, it is. Now, we just have to prove he meant it."

CHAPTER 10

When Debbie and I arrived at my parents' to an empty house, I sighed in relief. Our discussion with Bubba had been almost as disturbing as the way he lived.

"I feel like I have bugs crawling all over me," Debbie said, heading for the stairs. "I'm going to grab that shower right now."

After plopping down on the couch, I closed my eyes and tried to forget the pigsty Bubba wallowed in and concentrate on what he'd said.

Well, if I couldn't have her, no one should, right?

Textbook psychopath boyfriend if I'd ever heard it, and just like that, Bubba went directly to the top of my suspect list.

However, it was too easy.

Bubba was a simple man. He didn't seem to care about the basic comforts of life like air conditioning, showers, or the cleanliness of his home. He obviously enjoyed beer a great deal, and although his idea of love seemed skewed, he had treasured Kara. But to what extent? Enough to kill her if she decided to move on, which would have firmly set him in the psycho territory? Or did he not understand the weight of his words, what they had implied?

Again, it was too easy to blame him for the murder, but I couldn't help it. I still had other people to interview, which exhausted me. Frankly, my home called to me. I missed Tinker and Belle, my cozy house, my boss, Harold, my sweet, little town… and I even longed to see Minnie and her snotty cows and Tinker's stupid chickens. I loved being with my parents, but this wasn't my life. I wanted to go *home*.

When the pipes had burst in the old Rupert home in December, Derek and I had decided to redo the house, and the construction had been finished right before we'd arrived in Louisiana. We needed to put that house on the market. His personal home still sat empty, and we'd decided to rent it. We had a lot of balls up in the air in California and thinking about them stressed me out.

Carla and Max had agreed to take care of Tinker,

Belle, and the chickens while we were in Louisiana, but I assumed they wished we'd return soon as well. Belle wasn't very social and I hoped she and their cat, Francis, didn't fight too much.

But, I couldn't go anywhere. Not until Sheriff Brewer assured me that Hank was off his radar for the murder. And with their history, I wasn't sure I'd ever believe it. I needed to catch the killer and put the whole debacle to rest.

Debbie trotted down the stairs, running her hand through her red hair. "I thought I'd never wash the grime from that horrid place off me," she said, sitting in the chair. "You better head up before you find mold or something growing on your legs."

"I know," I replied. "I'm tired, Debbie. I don't think I can move right now, and I want to go home."

"Girl, I hear you. It's been fun, but it's time to get back to real life."

"Is Carla holding everything together?"

"Of course she is, but she said she needs me to come back."

"Well, you should talk to the sheriff. He can't hold you here for no reason." I stood up and stretched my arms over my head. "I'm going to get that shower."

WE NEVER MADE it out to dinner. The motor trouble with Hank's friends' boat had been far more complicated than anyone expected, and they didn't arrive back at the house until after dark. Mama made meatloaf and mashed potatoes and we opened a bottle of wine. Meanwhile, Debbie and I told everyone of our visit to Bubba's apartment.

"That poor girl," Mama said, shaking her head. "To live in such squalor and to have to take care of a man like that."

"Awful," Hank agreed. "Old Bubba should be ashamed of himself."

"What about your trip to the bakeries?" Mama asked. "How did that go?"

Debbie and I exchanged glances when a thumping sound came from outside the kitchen. We all turned toward the sliding glass door. I fully expected to find someone standing behind the glass, but there was nothing but darkness. Creepy, but a nice diversion from my mom's question.

"Must be one of the trees on the side of the house," Mama said, her gaze sliding over to Hank.

He nodded, but his brow furrowed, as if he were unsure if he believed that or not.

"Anyway," I continued, "tomorrow I'm going to

visit Cathy over at Cathy's Catering and hear what she has to say."

"How are you going to approach her?" Derek asked.

"Well, I thought I'd approach her as a woman who wants to get married."

He laughed and squeezed my hand. "Do you need your groom to go with you?"

"That would be great. Thanks for the offer."

"When are you two going to tie the knot?" Hank asked.

Derek and I exchanged glances, and I shrugged. "When the sheriff doesn't want to put any of us away for Kara's death."

I'd shared my thoughts on the target being on Hank with Derek and Debbie, but kept it from my mom and the man himself. They tended to worry, and I frankly didn't have any concrete evidence—just a hunch—but I'd learned to trust those hunches because so far, they'd served me well in my unfortunate murder investigations.

"The evidence will lead to the true murderer," Hank said firmly as another thumping sound came from outside. "You'll see."

"We need to do something about that tree," Mama

said through gritted teeth. "I heard it last night as well."

Hank nodded absently while taking a sip of his tea and bourbon. Something seemed to be troubling him, but I couldn't imagine what. The problem with the boat? Perhaps he and my mom got into a fight? Hadn't Edna the psychic said Mom and Hank would go through some rough times? It seemed another one of her predictions was coming true.

"The meatloaf's delicious, Jennifer," Debbie said as she patted her mouth with her napkin. "I had time this afternoon to make a chocolate cake if anyone is interested."

I narrowed my gaze on her, wondering if she'd had a chance to make me something sugar-free while she whipped up her delicacies.

"Relax. It's sugar-free," Debbie said, rolling her eyes.

"That's too bad," Hank said. "I'm not very partial to sugar-free. I prefer the real deal."

"Trust me," Debbie replied, standing. "You won't be able to tell the difference. If your daughter hadn't been giving me the evil eye, I wouldn't have mentioned it."

"Do you really think Cathy's Catering had

anything to do with Kara's murder?" Mama asked while we cleared away the plates.

"I don't know," I answered with a shrug. "Maybe? It's my understanding that she's been trying to move into Francois' territory for a bit now. What better way than to have someone die at one of his weddings?"

"It just seems so... I don't even know the word for it."

"Cutthroat?" Derek asked.

"Exactly," Mama said. "If she is responsible, she's going to extremes and frankly, I don't know if Francois' business will be touched by Kara's death. He's a permanent fixture in this town, like one of the statues. The only reason we were able to secure him for your wedding was because I go to church with him. I'm sorry to say, but it's going to take much more than a woman being killed for people to stop calling him."

Another sound came from outside, but this time, it resembled a chair being dragged across the deck.

"What was that?" Debbie asked as Hank stood.

"I'll check it out," he murmured. "But I have a feeling I know what it is."

Mama placed her elbows on the table and her head in her hands.

"What's wrong?" I asked when the sliding door closed behind Hank and Derek.

"Nothing. Let's wait and hear what Hank says."

I followed them outside and glanced around. The crescent moon hung high in the sky and didn't provide much of a glow.

"This here used to be over here," Hank said, pointing at the yellow and white deckchair. "It's been moved."

He shined a flashlight around the yard. A chill crept up my spine while I tried to recall the last place I'd seen it. Had someone moved it? But who? Or was Hank merely confused and mistaken?

I followed the beam of light, searching behind trees for our furniture mover, imagining them hidden and in fits of giggles as we talked about the chair. Maybe it was the same person who had laid out the fish for Irwin and cut the speaker wire. But why continue to mess with us?

Anger ignited within me. "Whoever you are, come out! Now!"

I was met with silence as we quietly traipsed through the yard.

Irwin's bathtub lay empty, his little yellow rubber ducks floating on the surface. I glanced down at the water's edge, finding nothing but darkness. Where was he?

We rounded the corner to where the tree had been thumping. I gasped and my heart skipped a few beats when I realized there weren't any trees on this side of the house—where Kara had died.

"Was it the gate making all that noise?" Derek whispered next to me. "There aren't any trees around."

"I... I don't know," I murmured.

Hank walked ahead of us. Derek and I exchanged glances as footsteps approached us from behind. My heart seemed to leap into my throat, and we turned to find Mama and Debbie walking toward us.

"What's going on?" Debbie asked as thunder rumbled in the distance. She glanced over her shoulder toward the black expanse that led down to the water. "I feel like I've just entered a horror flick."

It was a perfect description. My hands shook and my heart thundered while I waited for the psychopath with a chainsaw to jump out at us.

"Mama, what's happening?" I asked. "Why did Hank say it was the trees hitting the house when it's pretty obvious to me now that there aren't any trees on this side?"

"Let's wait and see what he has to say," Mama said

again, but I noted the worry on her face as she chewed her lip.

The glow of the flashlight illuminated Hank and the fence. He pushed on the gate and shined the light on the lock, then walked the line and pulled on each board. He stepped back and scratched his head, then turned and sauntered back toward us.

I felt someone behind me and glanced over my shoulder, fully expecting to find Derek. Instead, I stared into the darkness, yet I couldn't shake the feeling that someone, or something, was *right there*. I squinted into the night, sure I was losing my mind.

Hank returned to us shaking his head.

"What's going on?" Derek asked.

"I think she's still here," Hank replied.

"Who's still here?" I asked, glancing around, my stomach tossing and turning because I had an idea of where the conversation was leading.

"Kara."

Silence settled between us while Hank glanced around the yard again.

"You think... Kara, the woman who was killed, is... still here?" Derek asked.

"I do," Hank replied. "I think her life was taken so quickly and violently, she didn't make it to the other side. We've got to help her make the trip."

"And how do we do that?" Debbie asked.

"Well, I'll need to call someone who specializes in such things," Hank said, stroking his beard.

We all turned as a loud hiss filled the air. Irwin rounded the corner of the house and ran toward us.

"I haven't seen him move that fast in years," Hank muttered as he pushed us against the side of the house, clearing a path for the gator. But we held no interest to Irwin for he scooted past us to the back fence, growling as he went.

When he reached the area where Kara had been killed, he stopped and stared at the fence as if he'd cornered his prey. He roared and bellowed, obviously terribly unhappy about something.

"See? Even Irwin knows she's here," Hank said. "We need to help that poor girl."

CHAPTER 11

It was hard trying to sleep when there was a ghost outside the house. Thankfully, her bumping around didn't continue into the night. Hank had said she heard that we were going to get help for her and now, she'd wait patiently. He and Mama had talked late into the night in hushed tones, and I had the distinct feeling they were arguing.

The sunlight streaming through the window was a glorious sight. Louisiana during the nighttime hours could be scary, but after what I'd witnessed, I had become downright terrified and barely slept a wink. Derek had tossed and turned next to me, but we didn't speak. I had a feeling he was a little freaked out as well.

By the time I went downstairs for some coffee, Hank had left for work. Mama sat in the kitchen by herself, staring out the sliding glass door with her forehead pinched in worry.

"Are you okay?" I asked as I poured myself a cup.

"Yes, I'm fine. A little rattled, but I'm okay."

"That's understandable. Last night was scary. What's Hank's plan to help Kara?"

"He wants to bring in a Voodoo priestess, while I think we should have our pastor come over."

Now I understood the hushed, angry tones I'd heard. Mama believed Voodoo was evil, while Hank had grown up with it his whole life and considered it another religion. I'd learned bits and pieces growing up and found the religion fascinating. "Are you afraid the priestess is going to invite bad spirits in?"

"Yes. Perhaps the pastor can release Kara's soul without all the Voodoo nonsense."

"Maybe you can have both come over?" I asked. "We all want the same thing."

"You're right," Mama said, smiling. "Such the diplomat. I'll go see Pastor Matthew today and ask if he'd be willing to help us out."

"Derek and I are going to Cathy's Catering," I said.

"Please be careful."

"What's she going to do? Beat me with a spatula?"

"You never know. Caterers also have knives and silver trays. In the movies when someone gets hit with a tray, they always go down."

We giggled as Debbie came in. "What's so funny?"

"Just being silly," Mama said. "What's on your agenda today?"

"Carla and I are having a Facetime call in a few minutes so I can walk her through the recipe for the strawberry donuts. Apparently, I made a grocery list on the recipe card and she became confused on what ingredients were actually supposed to go into the donuts and what ingredients were merely on the list. She had to throw away the whole batch, so we're going to go over it and have her write out a new recipe card which, according to Carla, I shall not touch. Ever."

"That's too bad," Mama said. "Such a waste."

"Yeah, it's my fault. Me being here has only proven that I need to get more organized. I can't keep everything filed away in my noggin and expect to rely on others."

I sipped my coffee as I stared at Debbie. She'd always been a control freak until Carla had started working for her. They'd joined together in partnership, and I was happy to hear Debbie realizing the error of her ways. It also solidified that she needed to get home.

"Sheriff Brewer called this morning," Mama said. "He'll be coming over later this afternoon and asked that everyone be present."

"Maybe they've found the killer," Debbie replied. "Wouldn't that be great?"

"It sure would," Mama agreed. "You kids need to get back to your lives."

Was she tired of having us around? Perhaps. What was supposed to have been a happy occasion had sure brought a lot of stress and drama into her home. Frankly, if I were her, I'd want all of us gone, as well.

Derek hurried into the kitchen and grabbed a mug, then filled it with coffee. He smiled at me, but I noted the stress around his eyes. The fallout from our wedding was taking its toll on everyone.

We all chatted for a few moments, then Debbie headed back upstairs, Mama left for the church, and Derek and I loaded up in the rental car to head to Cathy's. Forty-five minutes later, we arrived at a quaint pink building with arched windows just outside of New Orleans proper.

"We're just going to play it like we're looking for a caterer and not let her know that we've already had one wedding destroyed by murder, right?"

I met Derek's gaze and nodded. "Yup. Like that never happened. We're in the planning stages of getting married and shopping around."

"Let's see what she's got to say," Derek said with a sigh.

A little bell sounded as we opened the door. The catering office consisted of two pink high back chairs and one green couch. Pictures of food and weddings lined the walls. A woman hurried out from the back, smiling. Short with a blonde bob, she stared at us over the glasses perched on the tip of her nose.

"How can I help you two?" she asked.

"We're looking for Cathy," I said.

"That's me. What can I do for you?"

I noted her crisp dialect and realized she was a transplant, not a local. She had none of the drawl usually detected from those born and bred in Louisiana.

"We're getting married," Derek said, laying his arm across my shoulders and pulling me close to him. "We're looking for a caterer."

"Wonderful!" Cathy exclaimed while she clapped her hands together. "Congratulations! Is this your second marriage?"

Derek and I exchanged glances. Yes, he was forty and the magical number lay right around the corner for me, but I found the question rude.

"I ask to get an idea of budgets," Cathy said. "Most first-timers are looking for a huge, elegant meal, while those moving into their second or third marriages aren't."

"It's our first," Derek said.

"Wow! You both waited a long time to find the right one, didn't you?" Cathy said with a laugh. I didn't appreciate her comments about our ages.

"Yes, we did," Derek said, smiling. "It took many years for me to find this gem."

"Well, let's sit down and look over some meal plans," Cathy said. "When's the big day?"

"Next month," I replied.

"My goodness! You sure are in a hurry to get to the altar! Is there a late-in-life baby on board?"

"No," I said, now gritting my teeth. This woman seemed to have no boundaries.

"Is the date going to be a problem?" Derek asked as he led me over to the couch. "The other caterer we spoke to said it shouldn't be an issue."

"No, no. Of course not," she said, picking up her

pen and paper from the coffee table. "We can make something work."

"Okay, great!" Derek exclaimed. "We're sure looking forward to it."

"What other caterers did you see?" Cathy asked.

"Francois over at Francois' Fancy Food Catering," I replied.

"He was really nice," Derek said. "But we are on a budget and we wanted to shop around a bit."

"Of course." Cathy gave a false smile, her jaw tight. Even the mention of her competitor's name irritated her almost as much as she irritated me. "He's quite expensive, and there are some other issues you'll run into by using him. I'm glad you came to me."

Dropping that little bomb and leaving it was a nice touch, and invited questioning.

"What does that mean?" Derek asked.

"Oh, it's nothing," Cathy said, waving her hand. "Just some things I've heard."

"Well, we'd like to hear about them as well," I said. "Our wedding is very important and we need to make good choices on who we use. I don't want to be a stressed-out mess on the day I get married. I want the ceremony to go smoothly and if you have information that could help facilitate that, we would greatly appreciate you sharing it."

A giggle almost escaped at the audacity of my words. My wedding day had already gone into the books as one of the worst I'd personally ever heard of.

"Well, I'm not one to gossip…"

The people who said that were the ones who chatted the most, so I smiled and waited expectantly.

"Please, tell us what you know," Derek urged.

"Well, he's terribly overpriced," Cathy said, lowering her voice conspiratorially. "For what he charges, he should be using premium, organic food."

"He said he does," I said, furrowing my brow. "That's what he told us."

"To further his profit margins!" Cathy exclaimed. "He claims to use organic and charges higher prices, but then he doesn't and pockets the difference. He's a true scam artist."

Derek and I exchanged glances and it took everything in my power not to roll my eyes. Cathy was proving the rumors true: she really had it out for Francois.

"He's been around forever," Derek said, shaking his head. "How has he gotten away with that for so long?"

"Uneducated customers," Cathy replied. "Unfortunately, most people trust their caterer, and they shouldn't. It's so easy to pull the wool over their eyes."

I furrowed my brow, thoroughly confused. "Are you saying we shouldn't trust you?"

"Oh, no!" Cathy said with a laugh, her cheeks turning red. "That's not what I meant. I'm honest, so you can definitely trust me."

"Just not Francois," I said.

"Exactly. He's a slippery one."

Derek and I gazed at her, waiting for her to continue.

"He's not very nice to his employees," she blurted with a sniff while she pushed her glasses up her nose. "The stories I could tell about him losing his temper with them. He's not a good man."

"He seems very sweet," I murmured.

"Of course he does. You're the ones lining his pockets! He's not going to show his true colors to you." Cathy stared at us a moment as if to gauge whether she'd said enough to damage Francois' reputation. "Let's get back to your menu. Tell me what you'd like."

"Well, I'm Italian, so I'd definitely like to stick to

that theme," Derek said. "Lots of pasta, rich sauces and of course, a bunch of garlic bread."

"How am I supposed to kiss you if you smell like garlic?" I asked, turning to him. He grinned and squeezed my hand. His eyes glittered with mischief and I realized he was enjoying our little charade. I'd be surprised if he had one drop of Italian blood in him.

"I think we can manage," he said. "Maybe I'll carry some mints."

"Aren't you two sweet," Cathy said. "Italian food it is. Let me run in back and pull out some past menus I've put together."

"And tiramisu!" I called out to her as she hurried into the back.

"I hate tiramisu," Derek grumbled.

"We all have to make some compromises in this wedding," I whispered.

"I feel like we already have," Derek said. "I just want to find the killer and marry my bride."

"Me, too," I said. "And get home to start our new lives. Or go back to the old one. We were living together and everything so it was like we were married."

"Yes, it was. But I'd like to make it official."

Cathy returned and we feigned interest in her

pictures and menus. The photos of weddings she'd done in the past were pretty, but they couldn't compare to Francois'. Even the dish of noodles I'd seen looked better than her most elegant shots. It had been like he'd taken each noodle and placed it in the serving tray to create a beautiful pile of carbs.

"This is so pretty," I gushed while staring at a picture of a red plate overflowing with gnocchi covered in white and crimson sauce. But it wasn't—maybe average at best. It lacked a certain pizzazz that seemed to come naturally to Francois' dishes.

"We can certainly include double garlic in there if you'd like," Cathy said, her face beaming with pride.

"Well, we have a lot to think about, don't we honey?" Derek said, getting to his feet. "Thank you so much for your time."

"You're very welcome," Cathy said. "You know, one last thing that I heard about Francois…"

Her voice trailed off as if uncertain if she should continue. However, I smiled encouragingly, knowing full well she'd rake that poor man over the coals and then set him on fire if it meant stealing business from him.

"What's that?" Derek asked.

"He did a wedding last week, and one of his employees was murdered," Cathy said.

"Oh, my," I exclaimed. "How horrible!"

"Murdered how?" Derek asked.

"Well, it's my understanding there was a mix up at the wedding. The bride and groom received the wrong meal, which in itself is inexcusable."

"Getting the incorrect meal is certainly a shame, but someone died, which pales in comparison. What happened?" Derek asked.

"One of his employees was stabbed… she had a knife in her chest while she was sitting in the front seat of the catering van."

I gasped and brought my hand to my mouth. A heavy silence settled around us for a few seconds.

"It was the same employee who'd delivered the wrong meal. If Francois were so upset that he would kill a poor girl, do you really want him catering your wedding?"

CHAPTER 12

When we arrived home, Bernie sat on the sofa talking with Mama and Debbie. Hank was still at work, and would be home soon.

"They told me what you've been doing!" Bernie exclaimed as she embraced me. "Spill it! What happened with Cathy? Oh, my gosh! This is so darn exciting! Nothing like this ever happens in Arizona!"

Derek and I recounted the story while everyone listened intently.

"I'm fuming that she said those things about Francois," Mama murmured. "Absolutely fuming. I have half a mind to go over there and tell her my thoughts."

"She's trying to get business, that's all." I replied.

"She should be touting her own personal strengths instead of tearing down Francois, but she's not."

"Oh, she makes me mad," Mama said.

"Please don't get angry. Your blood pressure will go up and you know that can make you feel sick."

Shaking her head, she twisted her fingers into a fist. "It should be illegal to tell such awful lies. That woman is going straight to Hell."

"It's okay, Mama," I said, placing my hand on her forearm. "We know they're lies and Francois is going to be just fine. Cathy's plates look like dogfood next to his."

A bit of an exaggeration, but hopefully it would help to calm her down.

"She's definitely good at placing doubt in people's minds about Francois," Debbie said. "But honestly, she took it too far. It borders on ridiculousness."

"Or psychosis," I said. "She's definitely got it out for the poor man."

"But can someone who lies actually murder someone?" Derek asked.

"I would assume so," Bernie replied. "She sounds like she's a few cards short of a full deck, if you know what I mean."

"That's a big jump," I said.

Bernie shrugged. "To me, she's definitely a

contender for the murderer. If she's willing to tell outright lies, then she'd most likely be fine sticking a knife in a girl's chest."

"I don't know," Debbie said, chewing her lip. "Can someone really stoop to killing someone in order to destroy a business?"

"It's possible," Bernie replied. "Desperate people do desperate things."

We sat in silence for a few minutes as we tried to digest the weight of our discussion.

"What do you think, Tilly?" Debbie asked. "Do you like Cathy better than Bubba as the killer?"

"Who's Bubba?" Bernie asked.

After I gave her the rundown on him, she stared at me wide-eyed. "Wow. You've been busy doing everything but actually getting married!"

"That is so true," I said with a sigh. "But I've got to find the killer."

"Bubba or Cathy?" Debbie asked again.

"Don't forget Russo," Derek said.

"And who's that?" Bernie asked.

"The former mob guy from the Northeast who squealed on the mob," Derek said. "In return, he got federal protection and is supposed to be living a quiet life down here."

Bernie furrowed her brow. "And he's not?"

"Not really," I replied. "He was furious over the food mix up at the wedding. The groom said he tried to break up with Russo's daughter, but Russo broke into his apartment and threatened if he didn't marry her, he'd take him out to the Gulf of Mexico and drop him in the water tied to cement blocks."

"Holy cow!" Bernie exclaimed. "He's definitely the guy!"

I shrugged and shook my head. "I don't know, Bernie. We can guess all day long, but until we have proof or better yet, a confession, we can't pinpoint who it is."

"Well he sure hasn't reformed in any way," Bernie said. "That's mob tactics 101 right there."

"He could definitely stomach giving a kill order to some schmuck," Debbie agreed. "He's probably responsible for lots of deaths. Didn't Francois say he used to be a mob enforcer?"

"Something like that," Derek said.

"There are a lot of excellent suspects," Bernie mused. "It seems that everyone has a reason to kill Kara, and unfortunately, she's an innocent victim, even a pawn, in every single scenario."

"You're right," I said with a nod. "We haven't really looked at who in Kara's life would want to kill her, except her lovely boyfriend, Bubba."

"If I can't have her, no one will!" Debbie shrieked, then cackled manically while rubbing her hands together like an evil scientist bringing a monster to life.

"Now that you mention that part, I think it's him," Bernie said. "Definitely the boyfriend."

As everyone discussed the options for the killer, I mused about whether I was looking for one or two people: the idiot who had ruined my wedding and the killer. I still didn't have a definitive answer.

A knock sounded at the door and Mama rose to open it. Sheriff Brewer stood on the other side. With a grin, he tipped his hat. "Hello, Jennifer."

"Sheriff! Come in, come in!" she said. "Can I get you some tea?"

"No, ma'am. Thank you though. I actually came here to talk to your daughter."

My stomach churned and then proverbially sank to my knees. I'd learned that a sheriff wanting to talk to me never meant anything positive.

"Of course," Mama said. "Tilly, you remember Sheriff Brewer?"

"How could I forget?" I replied, standing. "It's nice to see you again."

Pants on fire. I may burn in hell for that lie.

"Is there somewhere private we can talk?" he asked, his grin still in place as we shook hands.

"We can go out back," I said. "It's a pretty afternoon. Shouldn't be too hot with all the cloud cover and breeze."

Without another word, I turned and headed for the kitchen to the back door, not giving him a chance to answer. Maybe Irwin would be hanging outside and give Brewer a little chase. I'd like to witness that.

As we settled into the chairs, I glanced around the yard and found Irwin resting in his bathtub, a rubber duck in his mouth.

"I see Hank is still messing around with that gator," Brewer said. "They make better boots than they do pets. I've seen firsthand what they're capable of doing to human flesh. Foolish old man."

"He's no older than you," I said. Our gazes locked and he stared me down for a minute, then I looked away. The guy had an intimidating glare. "What can I do for you?"

"Well, as I do with all my cases, I've been conducting some background research on everyone involved, and I wanted to discuss your past."

My heart skipped a beat while I stared at Irwin, not liking where the conversation was leading.

"I called the Oak Peak Sheriff's office and spoke to Connor," Brewer continued. "Seems that you've had some problems at home."

With a grin, I slid my gaze over to Brewer. The problem was that Connor couldn't catch a murderer if they stood in front of him holding a blinking sign identifying themselves as the killer. I'd done him a bunch of favors, and now he'd trash-talked me. I could feel it. "Please tell me what the esteemed Oak Peak Sheriff had to say."

"Well, apparently you like intimidating people with baseball bats."

I burst out laughing so hard, I gave myself a case of the snorts. Sounding like a little piglet wasn't the calm, mature persona I had hoped to portray. "I thought my neighbor's house was being robbed. And by the way, I'm marrying the guy I threatened."

He raised an eyebrow at me. "What about getting yourself caught up in murder investigations that are none of your business?"

"Well, if the sheriff had made an attempt to find the true murderer instead of accusing me and those I care about of such awful crimes, then I wouldn't have to stick my nose where it doesn't belong."

Brewer chuckled and shook his head. "You're

something else, Tilly Bordeaux. You remind me a bit of your mama when she was younger."

I smiled, thinking that we'd finally be able to agree on something. Mama was terrific, and if I resembled her in any way, shape or form, he couldn't think too badly of me.

"Especially when it comes to making poor decisions," Brewer said, his smile fading.

"What does that mean?"

"Your mama chose a loser over law enforcement, and it seems as if you're doing the same."

"Hank isn't a loser," I said. "He's far from it."

"He rides around in a boat telling stories all day," Brewer said through gritted teeth. "That's a loser."

I rolled my eyes and shook my head as I attempted to keep my anger under control. "Do you have anything else you want to say to me besides calling my father names?"

Brewer shrugged while a grin crawled across his face. "Well, besides talking to the Sheriff of Oak Peak, I also spoke to a nice, young man who works for him—Deputy Byron Mills. He said the two of you used to date, that you had a great thing going, just like Jennifer and I did. Then, a stranger with a very shady past moved to town and swept you off your feet. Poor Byron said it was like he didn't even exist any longer."

Oh, my goodness. How the truth had been bent and distorted. Was Byron losing his dang mind? "It's not any of your business, but there was nothing 'great' about my dates with Byron Mills. The guy bored me to tears. The relationship was over before it ever began."

"That's not the way he remembered it. A love story for the ages was the way he told it. He said something happened to change your mind about him. In fact, he alluded that you're most likely on drugs, like your groom in there."

I tried not to lose my temper. I truly did, but it didn't quite work out that way. Standing from my chair, it crashed to the deck. I placed my hands on the table between us and said, "Byron Mills is an idiot and so are you. I can plainly see that my mama made the right decision when she chose Hank over you. You are a sorry excuse for a man, and an absolutely pathetic excuse for a sheriff."

It would have been an excellent idea to stop there, but my frustrations over my wedding, the murder, and the sorry simp overflowed. "Is it a requirement in law enforcement to be dumb as a bag of rocks in order to serve?"

"How dare you!" Sheriff Brewer yelled, also getting to his feet. He must have startled Irwin, because the gator roared and climbed out of his bathtub. "You listen to me, you smart-mouthed, disrespectful little woman... I am this close to finding the killer and I'll be making an arrest soon. I told your mama all those years ago that Hank was bad news, and I'm finally going to be able to prove it to her."

Out of the corner of my eye, I noted Irwin sauntering over.

"I saw that one coming a mile away," I said through gritted teeth, and briefly wondered if I should warn him that Irwin was mere feet from him. "And I'm way ahead of you on this investigation, Sheriff."

Just then, Hank stepped out the back door and stared at the scene unfolding in front of him. His eyes widened and he yelled, "Get, Irwin! I don't know what you have up your sleeve, but it ain't happening today!" Hank set himself between the sheriff and the gator, waving his arms. "Go on!"

I knew running interference with Brewer and Irwin was the right thing for him to do, but at the moment fury roiled through me and I actually enjoyed the thought of Irwin taking a chunk out of the smug jerk.

Brewer turned around to glance back at me. "He's going down," he whispered. "I'm going to make sure of it."

CHAPTER 13

The next night, Bernie came over for the expelling of Kara's spirit. The moon hung high in the sky, casting its glow all around the yard. A light breeze wafted through the trees, and overall, it would have been a perfect night to gather for a glass of wine in the backyard, tell stories and laugh.

But Kara needed to find peace, and Hank had brought in the big guns to help her.

"I wouldn't miss this for the world," Bernie whispered to me as we stood in the backyard watching the Voodoo priestess set bowls of sage around the side of the house. Her long, flowing blue dress seemed almost ghostly against her black-as-night skin, and she had the most beautiful ocean-blue eyes

I'd ever seen. "Nothing strange like this happens in Arizona."

"Not in California, either," I said, also keeping my tone low, but I wasn't sure why. It just seemed like the right thing to do. The priestess was getting ready to send someone to their final resting place, and it was a somber, serious moment. Maybe even a bit like a funeral.

"The wild west is boring compared to home, isn't it?" Bernie asked with a sigh.

I nodded and crossed my arms over my chest. "Yes, but I'm ready to go back to my dull life in my little town."

"You'll find the killer soon," Bernie said. "I have complete faith in you."

"Thanks," I said with a grin. "I wish I shared your confidence."

"You will," she reiterated. "But I do have to admit, I've loved hanging out with you. We need to do a better job of keeping in touch, Tilly."

"I agree." I sighed. "We used to be so close."

"And there's no reason we can't be close again."

Debbie, Hank, Derek and Mama walked out of the house, trailed by the pastor who was supposed to have married me. In his seventies, he shuffled over slowly, keeping his gaze firmly on the ground. The bald spot on his head glowed under the moon and he wore a cervical collar which rested on his clerical one, indicating his accident had been a little more serious than he had let on.

Hank wandered over and talked to the woman getting ready for the ceremony. They exchanged hugs and grins. The smiles eventually faded and they slid into deep conversation. Meanwhile, I met the pastor.

"TILLY," he said after Mama introduced us. "I'm Pastor Matthew, and I'm so sorry I wasn't able to officiate the wedding."

"It's fine," I said. "The day was a disaster and we wouldn't have been able to get married anyway, thanks to the gator and a slew of other issues."

"The gator?"

I glanced over at her and she shook her head. "Mama didn't tell you about Irwin?"

"No, she didn't."

After I explained the story, I realized it had probably been a blessing in disguise that the pastor had been in an accident. He didn't move fast, and Irwin could be very unpredictable. If he decided he didn't like someone, he'd rush them, and the pastor wouldn't have had a prayer of getting away. He'd have far worse injuries than some whiplash... like missing flesh.

"Oh, my," Pastor Matthew murmured. "And a murder on top of it."

"Yes. The whole day was quite alarming," Mama said with a faraway look in her eye as if the memory left her shell-shocked. "Absolutely awful."

Her comment made me wonder if she held more remorse for my wedding day than I did.

"Well, if you decide to tie the knot, I'd like to offer my services."

"Thank you," I said in a noncommittal tone. After I'd found the murderer, I liked the idea of Debbie marrying us. It became much more personal for our friend to make us official instead of a stranger.

"I see Roseline is here," Matthew said. "I haven't seen her in ages."

"You know her?" Mama asked, her eyes wide in surprise.

"Oh, yes. Lovely woman."

"I thought practicing Voodoo was considered evil in the Christian faith," Mama said, her brow furrowed in confusion.

"Some may think so, but once it's been studied, it really isn't. When the African slaves were brought to our country, they carried their Voodoo religion with them. Of course, slave owners wanted them to practice Christianity. The slaves took some elements and combined them with their own. As carrier of God's word, who am I to judge others' religion?"

I appreciated the man's line of thought. Even though I'd never practiced any set religion, I did consider myself spiritual.

"Most religions on our great planet all want the same thing," Pastor Matthew continued. "They want peace and the ability to raise families in a safe environment. Whatever God they pray to, whatever their religious practices, it doesn't matter... unless, of course, they are hurting others. I actually find Voodoo a very powerful and beautiful religion."

He then shuffled toward Roseline, and the two greeted each other with open arms and smiles, like two good friends who hadn't seen each other in a long time.

"And here I worried Pastor Matthew would be upset at Hank bringing in a Voodoo Priestess," Mama said. "We've been arguing about it for days. Shoot, was I wrong about that one."

So, she and Hank *had* been fighting, just as Edna the psychic had predicted. She had definitely been the real deal.

"You certainly were," Bernie agreed, giving my mom a hug. "I can't wait to see the ceremony."

Thunder roiled in the distance and we all glanced up at the sky. "Hopefully we won't get rained out," Derek murmured.

"No kidding," I said. "Kara needs to find her peace. We can't put that off on account of rain."

Hank sauntered over and asked Derek to help him gather some chairs and a pile of firewood. A few moments later, they'd built a bonfire in the grass and placed the chairs around it.

"Please take your places," Roseline said, the Haitian accent thick. Her gaze glittered with friendliness as she motioned us toward the chairs. I sat between Bernie and Derek and we all glanced at each other nervously.

"I think I'll wait inside," Debbie said, standing. "This is a little creepy for me."

"It would be greatly appreciated if you stayed," Roseline advised from the other side of the fire. "Your energy is quite positive and I can use it to help the poor girl to the other side."

"Shoot," Debbie whispered, plopping back down into the deckchair. "I don't like the feeling of this thing."

"Please take each other's hands," Roseline said as

she closed her eyes and stretched her fingers to her sides.

I glanced around the yard, then settled my palms in Derek's and Bernie's. The buckets of sage she'd set up had been lit, and the smoke wafted all around us, tickling my nose and throat while the bonfire burned brightly. I really hoped I wouldn't sneeze. Thankfully, I didn't see Irwin creeping up on us from behind. Hank had taken him down to the water earlier in the day and dumped a bunch of fish for him to eat, claiming the gator would stay put for a few days from overeating.

Roseline began to chant in a language I didn't recognize, her arms still out. Maybe Haitian? French? A little bit of both? After a few minutes, her rhythmic mantras lulled me into a state of relaxation. The tension in my neck loosened, my limbs felt heavy, and I fought against my eyelids fluttering closed.

"I feel weird," Bernie whispered. "Like I've been drugged."

"Same here," I murmured. "My body doesn't seem to want to move."

"My head's swimming. Like my brain has turned to mush."

The chanting continued as Roseline swayed.

Shortly after, she raised her hands above her head and slowly twirled in a circle. Her eyes opened wide and a bead of sweat tracked down her cheek. As she continued her unhurried dance, I noted she stared at everything yet never fixed her gaze on anything. She seemed to be deep in trance and I longed to understand what she was saying. An article on a Voodoo ceremony would most likely send the town folks of Oak Peak into an absolute tizzy, and I couldn't wait to write it. I wished I had my notebook, but I probably couldn't hold a pen, even if I tried. I attempted to wiggle my fingers, and they reminded me of hundred-pound blocks. Perhaps I could interview the priestess after the ceremony.

An icy chill swept over my skin when Hank slowly rose from his seat. His arms floated upward and he began to spin in a slow circle as well. I watched in fascination as he gracefully moved—a direct contradiction to his normal bull-in-a-china-shop gait. His eyes were also out of focus, looking everywhere, but not actually locking onto any particular thing.

"Oh, my word," Mama muttered. "Pastor, please pray for him."

"He's fine," Jennifer," Matthew said. "Relax. It's all part of the process. Open yourself to the experience."

Glancing over at mama, I noted her eyelids closed so tightly, they might as well have been screwed shut. She had no intention of opening herself up to the experience and couldn't wait for it to be over.

Debbie was the next to rise. Her dance wasn't nearly as graceful as Hank's. Instead, her limbs jerked and contorted in odd angles as more thunder rumbled in the distance.

"Roseline is in touch with the spirits, the *Loas*," Pastor Matthew said. "It's a beautiful dance of give and take between the spiritual world and the earthly plane."

"What's with Hank and Debbie?" Derek whispered.

"The spirits are moving them," Matthew said.

I didn't quite understand if the pastor meant the spirits had taken over their bodies, or that their presence had moved Hank and Debbie on a deep level. Not bothering to question him, I continued to stare, utterly captivated.

Roseline's chanting became louder, her movements more pronounced. A loud banging sound came from the side of the house, and I glanced over to find nothing there. It was the same noise we'd heard the night Hank had declared Kara's spirit trapped on this plane. She'd been quiet ever since, but apparently she'd now decided to make herself known.

Debbie continued to move in strange, almost comical ways, while Hank floated around with the grace of a ballerina. Thunder once again boomed in the distance.

"The storm is getting closer," Derek said.

"I know. Hopefully this will wrap up before we all end up soaked."

Bernie suddenly stood, her arms out to her sides. She had the same faraway look as the others. As she began to sway, Roseline's incantations reached a fever pitch. The wind picked up as more banging came from the side of the house. The flames burning the sage and the firepit flickered as if they tried to extinguish, but something kept them lit. Hank and Debbie continued their dances, and an icy chill crawled over my skin. I glanced over at Mama to find her head on the pastor's shoulder while she whispered a prayer.

For a brief second, time seemed to stop. The wind stilled, as did Hank, Debbie and Roseline. Bernie stood next to me, her eyes wide, but still not seeing anything. There was one last banging sound from the side of the house, and Roseline's body stiffened. Bernie's, too.

Thunder boomed right above us and a bolt of lightning lit up the night, striking Bernie and sending her to the ground.

CHAPTER 14

The lightning broke the spell. Mama screamed, Hank and Debbie glanced around as if unsure where they were, and Derek and I fell to our knees to help Bernie.

"Call 9-1-1!" Derek yelled as he felt for a pulse.

Completely paralyzed, my hands shook and tears cascaded down my cheeks. Was my cousin dead?

"She's got a heartbeat!' Derek yelled. Mama was calling emergency services. He leaned over her and placed his cheek centimeters from her face. "And she's breathing!"

Relief swept through me. I continued to cry, except they were happy tears. It seemed Bernie would be okay. Thank goodness Derek had his wits about him because I had become a useless mess, a feeling that had haunted me since my wedding day.

Bernie moaned and slowly moved her head from side to side.

Roseline came up beside us, a huge smile on her face. "I see the girl is well."

"Praise be," Pastor Matthew muttered. "Did you send Kara off?"

"Yes. She was very grateful for everyone being here."

"Excellent."

"Is she okay?" Hank asked, his brow furrowed in worry. He stared down at my cousin. Sirens wailed in the distance as Bernie groaned again.

"She's going to be fine," Roseline said. "Absolutely fine."

The priestess seemed so sure of herself, especially since she'd done nothing but glance at my cousin with a perceptive smile on her face. Had some message from the other side been presented to her? "How do you know?" I asked.

Roseline grinned and shook her head. "That is Bernie's journey to discover. I can assure you she'll be healthy once this passes."

More sirens screamed in the distance. They must have sent the calvary.

Bernie finally opened her eyes.

"We've called an ambulance," I said, taking her hand in mine. "I'm so glad you're okay!"

She stared at me, her face contorted in confusion. "What happened? One minute I was sitting in my chair, and now I'm on the ground."

"You were hit by lightning," I said. "It came out of the sky and zapped you as though Zeus threw the thunderbolt himself."

"Lightning!" she said, glancing upward. I followed her gaze and saw nothing but stars twinkling in the night sky. Where had the storm gone?

"Oh, my," she whispered. "I could have been killed!"

"Yes," I said, my throat tightening up once again. "You could have, and I'm so grateful you weren't."

"How do you feel?" Derek asked.

"Like I've been run over by a tractor-trailer going a hundred miles per hour," Bernie said, trying to sit up. "Everything hurts."

"Don't move," I said. "Please. Let the paramedics check you out before you try to get up."

Bernie lay back down and took some deep breaths, shutting her eyes.

"I'm going to take my leave," Roseline said to Hank. "My work here is finished."

"Thank you so much," Hank replied, drawing her into a big bear hug. "Let's not allow so much time to pass before we see each other again. I'd love to meet for coffee."

"I'd like that very much," Roseline said, turning to Mama. "As always, Jennifer, please take care of yourself."

The two women shook hands. Mama may not approve of Roseline and her religion, but she would always be polite to Hank's friends.

"May I drive you home, Roseline?" Pastor Matthew asked.

"I don't want to be a bother, Pastor."

"No bother, my dear," he said. "Your home is on the way, and I'd love the company."

"Then it would be my honor."

Mama and Hank escorted them out through the house while the rest of us stayed with Bernie. I looked over my shoulder to find Debbie standing behind me. "Are you okay?" I asked.

Debbie nodded. "Yep. Feel fine and dandy. A little confused like Bernie is, but I'm good."

"You sure can't dance," Derek teased.

"What does that mean?" Debbie asked, crossing her arms over her chest. "I don't dance. Ever. I've got two left feet. It isn't pretty."

"We noticed," Derek said, chuckling. My tears had dried up and I found myself laughing along with him.

"Explain yourselves," Debbie demanded.

When I tried to tell her what had happened, she shook her head. "Don't believe it. I'll need to see video in order to swallow that one."

Unfortunately, we had none to give her. Bernie coughed, and I turned my attention back to her. "You sure you're okay?"

She nodded and stretched her arms out. "I think so."

The sirens stopped in front of the house, and Hank hurried out to the back gate where Kara had died to let them in. Two men ran over with the gurney between them and motioned for us to clear away.

As I stood and stepped back, Derek placed his arm around my shoulder and I leaned into him, absolutely exhausted, both physically and mentally.

"I called my brother about Bernie," Hank said. "He wants to make sure she gets checked out at the hospital."

"It's a smart idea," Derek agreed. "It was a direct hit."

"Then it's a done deal," Hank said.

We all watched the paramedics work in silence.

"She's in pretty good shape for getting zapped," the first one said. "I can't find any burns on her."

"Yes, but we still need to take her in," the second one replied. "It looks like she may be suffering from some mild shock."

"Wouldn't you be? The sky just opened up on her. I know I'd be in shock as well."

"Man, shut up. Why do you have to be this way? I never said that we *shouldn't* bring her in, did I?"

The two bickered as they carefully moved Bernie over to the gurney and began to wheel it back toward the ambulance parked out front.

More sirens drew closer and stopped at the house. Mama came around the corner and laid her hand on my shoulder.

"They're a little late to this party," Debbie muttered.

Sheriff Brewer and two deputies stepped aside so the paramedics could move Bernie out. I groaned as he approached, wanting nothing more than to head to bed.

"What happened here?" he asked, not bothering with a greeting.

"Bernie was hit by lightning," Mama said. "It was terrifying, but they say she'll be fine."

"That's good," he said, glancing up at the sky. "Strange there isn't even a whisp of a cloud, though."

"You know how it is," Mama said. "The storms can roll through pretty quickly."

"Well, I'm glad she's going to make it," Brewer said. "But I'm afraid I've come with more bad news for tonight."

Mama groaned and shook her head. "What now?"

"Hank Bordeaux, I'm arresting you for the murder of Kara Lionheart."

Silence fell around us as we all stared at him. I knew this had been coming, but I couldn't get past the idea that I'd never known Kara's last name and I'd been so invested in finding her killer. Some super-sleuth I was.

"What the heck are you talking about, Marv?" Hank asked, shaking his head. "That's nonsense."

"You were the last one to see her," Brewer shot back. "And, your fishing knife was the murder weapon."

Hank's brow furrowed. "My fishing knife? I haven't seen that thing since a few days before Tilly arrived."

"Well, I recognize it, Hank. The one with gator carved into the hilt. There's only one like it around. You're always bragging about that, remember?"

"Sure I do," Hank said. "I had that carved by a guy who lives deep in the swamp. Paid him fifty bucks to do it. He's got some amazing skills. But like I said, I haven't seen that thing in almost a week."

"Spare me the innocent act," Brewer spat. "You're under arrest."

Mama stepped in front of Hank and placed her hands on her hips, tilting her chin upward. She'd been fairly quiet most of the week, but based on her body language, the sheriff was in for a tongue lashing. I almost felt sorry for him.

"What in tarnation is wrong with you, Marvin Brewer?" she yelled. "You aren't taking Hank anywhere, and he sure as heck didn't kill anyone! Quit being foolish and get yourself off my property!"

Brewer squared his shoulders and set his thumbs on top of his belt buckle as his two deputies stepped up on each side of him, all of them staring down my mom. "Now, listen here, Jennifer. We have Hank dead to rights. I told you from the beginning that this is a bad man, and now I've finally been able to prove it. He killed an innocent girl."

Mama shook her head, bit her lip and stared at the ground a few seconds before answering. Finally, she met his gaze and what I saw there scared me and caused the hair on the back of my neck to stand on end. It was the same stare she'd given me when I'd come home late from the prom at seventeen, and I'd been grounded for a month afterward. "Quit talking to me like I'm a dumb teenager, Marv," she hissed. "You and I both know Hank didn't murder that poor girl. I would bet my life on it."

"I wouldn't," the sheriff said with a shrug. "He's had trouble with the law before."

A collective gasp spread among Debbie, Derek and me and we all looked at my mom.

"That was when he was eighteen," she said through gritted teeth. "He's in his sixties now, you moron!"

"Oh, man," Debbie whispered as the sheriff hitched up his pants and the color drained from his cheeks. "This is going to be ugly."

"How dare you speak to law enforcement that way?" the deputy to Brewer's right said.

Mama stared him down until his shoulders sagged. "And how dare *you* come onto our property and accuse my husband of such horrendous crimes?"

She glared at Brewer again, and if she'd had Hank's knife, I had no doubt she'd bury it in his chest. Her cheeks flamed red and her mouth pinched into a fine line. "Leave," she whispered while pointing to the gate leading out to the front of the house. "And don't you even think about coming back here until you have the *real* criminal behind bars."

"N-now Jennifer, I can't do that," the sheriff said gently, not meeting her gaze, almost as if all his bluster had oozed out of him. "Hank's knife was the murder weapon."

"I'm about to murder you," Mama hissed. "Where's the shotgun, Hank?"

The two deputies drew their weapons and pointed them at my mom. Hank laid his hand on her shoulder and pulled her behind him while I stepped in front of her with my palms raised. "That's enough," I said.

"Yes, it is," Hank muttered. "You want to take me to jail for something I didn't do, then let's go, Marv. I've been in worse places."

Hank held his arms out in front of him, waiting for the cuffs. I stared down Brewer and his two idiot deputies as they holstered their weapons, then slapped the silver bracelets on Hank's wrists.

"How dare you!" Mama screamed. I grabbed her shoulders and held her back while she tried to claw out the sheriff's eyes.

"It's okay," I said, trying to soothe her, but I really wanted to let her go and have her way with him. "Hank will be fine."

Brewer pushed Hank forward and his deputies followed behind him.

"I love you!" Mama called.

The sheriff's shoulders sagged for a moment, but then he straightened them when he marched toward the gate.

"That rotten son of a—"

"Mama, it's going to be all right," I said. "Hank won't be in jail long."

I recalled Edna the psychic's reading on Mama.

"I see a few rough patches ahead for you... these times coming... they will be difficult, but it's important to remember that love you share for one another. It will keep you bonded, and it will carry over into your next life."

"Can you tell me what these rough patches are?" Mama had asked.

Edna had shaken her head. *"I don't know if it's illness, financial worries, or something else. The spirits won't elaborate. They just want you to stay the course, to remember the eternal love that brought you together."*

Mama turned to me, her eyes dry and her gaze hard. "You find out who really killed that girl, Tilly. You make sure Hank comes home to me, do you understand?"

I nodded solemnly and glanced over at Debbie

and Derek. They both stared at her wide-eyed, surprised by her outburst and moxie.

"Mama, I promise I'll find the killer," I vowed. "Please, try not to worry."

But what my next step would be in order to fulfill my marching orders, I had no idea. "Derek, did you ever call your lawyer?"

He nodded. "We were right. He doesn't practice in Louisiana, but he gave me the name of someone who does. Says she's like a Pitbull."

"We better call her," I said. "Hank's in a load of trouble, and we need all the help we can get."

esperate people do desperate things.

Bernie's words echoed in my head, and my whole body trembled with anxiety and despair. How was I going to prove Hank didn't murder Kara?

I tossed and turned most of the night, and finally gave up on sleep right before the sun came up and headed downstairs. Mama sat in the kitchen staring out the sliding glass door. Through the trees, the sky had begun to turn pink.

"Hi, honey," she said with a sad smile. "Did you sleep okay?"

"No," I replied with a sigh as I poured my coffee. "What about you?"

"Not a wink."

I sat down and followed her gaze out the window.

"Today, I need to visit Pastor Matthew," she said. "My mind is full of hateful thoughts of all the ways I want to kill Marv, and I need to clear them. I'm having trouble doing it myself."

"Okay. I'm going to talk to some people and see what I can find out about Kara."

"Thank you," she said, nodding. "Thank you for helping me through this. I'm a little embarrassed about my behavior last night, but that man—"

"Don't be," I said. "He's an idiot and they've got the wrong guy."

We sat in silence for a few moments, then Mama turned to me again. "What do you think about Hank's knife being the murder weapon?"

I shrugged and sipped my coffee. "I've been up all night trying to remember what the knife looked like when I found Kara. For the life of me, I can't recall. When did he have it made?"

"About four years ago," Mama said. "He was so proud of it and showed it to everyone who would listen to him wonder at the workmanship."

"I guess he told the sheriff about it."

"Apparently. I wasn't aware they still talked."

"I can't believe Brewer still holds a grudge against Hank for winning you over."

"It's ridiculous, isn't it?"

"It sure is."

"You would think that Hank would be able to sense it and steer clear of Marv, but you know how men are, especially your stepdad. It's impossible for him to pick up on things like that. He needs to be told outright and thinks everyone is like him. He just wants everyone to get along and be happy." Mama shook her head. "Silly men. Sometimes I don't think they ever grow up past the age of thirteen or so."

"Do you remember when Hank lost the knife?" I asked. "Where he was?"

The sky had turned flaming pink, and the birds began to sing. Daylight had arrived.

"A few days before you arrived," Mama said. "He searched all over the house that afternoon before he left for work. He couldn't find the darn thing anywhere and was terribly upset about it. Then, you and Derek arrived and our lives turned into this crazy whirlwind so he didn't mention it again. Most likely, he forgot he'd lost it."

"I wonder where it went," I muttered. "Where he misplaced it."

"Well, if someone used it as the murder weapon,

which I have my doubts, it would have to be outside somewhere. Unless one of our wedding guests came inside and suddenly found it even though Hank had practically torn the house apart looking for it."

"Why don't you think someone used it as a murder weapon?" I asked.

"Because it's a very different knife, Tilly. You would have noticed it."

"So you think the sheriff somehow got the knife and is now saying it's the murder weapon? What about the coroner? Wouldn't he have to agree?"

Mama shrugged and stood. "Marv and the coroner are good friends. He'd probably do anything Marv asked him to."

I didn't respond. There was a big difference between wishing ill on someone, like Brewer did to Hank, and bringing others in to set him up for the murder. Could the sheriff stoop that low?

"It's a possibility," Mama said. "I know you don't believe me, but Marv has been a jerk to your stepdad for years. Two years ago, he ticketed Hank for going three miles over the speed limit. Three miles, Tilly! Hank fought it and the judge threw it out. He also stopped one of Hank's swamp tours, demanding to see his business license, even though he knows Hank's been in business for years! It seems to me he's always got it out for Hank. I've always tried to be polite, but now, that man has gone too far."

"Well, it's definitely an interesting theory," I murmured, not sure what to really think about it.

"What are you doing today?" Mama asked, changing the subject. "What can we do to get Hank home?"

"I'm starting at the beginning," I said. "With Francois. Could he have killed Kara for the food mishap?"

"Doubtful," Mama said. "He doesn't have the stomach for it."

"How do you know for certain?"

Mama rolled her eyes. "He passed out during the church blood drive. He wasn't even getting his blood drawn—he was waiting in line to do so. When it was his turn and they called him in, he went down like a sack of rocks off a high building. After they revived him, he said he couldn't stand the sight of blood and needles."

"Well, he's a caterer, so I'm assuming he sees animal blood."

"For some reason that's different to him," Mama said. "I love Francois so I know I'm biased, but if he's got a killer bone in his body, I'm going to grow a rat tail and sprout wings."

The visual on that wasn't pretty. I sighed and

decided I needed to talk to Hank. The knife had become an important part of the investigation. If I could figure out where he'd lost it, that may lead to a new clue that would unravel this whole mess.

Would the sheriff allow me to meet with him, and should I take Mama with me?

No. Absolutely not. If she felt she had to go see Pastor Matthew today because of her violent thoughts toward Brewer, it would be best not to have them in the same room. I already had one parent in jail. I didn't need a second.

"Will they allow me to see Hank later today?" Mama asked, and I swore that sometimes she could read my mind.

"Maybe," I replied with a shrug. "You can't go in as angry as you were last night, though."

"Yes. That's why I want to go talk to Matthew today. I was thinking I'd stop by the jail on my way home this afternoon."

"You can give it a try." Meanwhile, I needed to scoot to the sheriff's office to get there before her and talk to Hank. "I'll see you later today, Mama."

I bent over and gave her a hug as tears welled in my eyes. "I feel like this is all my fault."

"Tilly!" she chastised, getting to her feet and

holding me at arms-length. "Don't be silly. You caused none of this!"

Deep down, I knew she was right, but I'd set the events in motion. "If I hadn't wanted to get married in Louisiana, Hank wouldn't be in jail, Kara wouldn't be dead, and you wouldn't be so upset."

Mama shook her head. "I absolutely loved that you wanted to come home to get married. I was so excited. Everything that has happened is just... coincidence. We'll get it all worked out. You need to quit talking like that."

"Okay," I replied, feeling slightly better.

"I'll see you later today," Mama said, kissing the tip of my nose. "I love you. Be safe."

I grabbed the keys to my rental car and beelined it for the jail.

"WHAT CAN I DO FOR YOU?" the woman behind the desk asked as we exchanged smiles. In her forties with shoulder-length black hair, she reminded me a bit of Bernie. If I had time, I'd stop by the hospital on my way home. I'd talked briefly to her while driving to the sheriff's office, and she'd been in great spirits.

"I'd like to see Hank Bordeaux," I said. "He was brought in last night."

Her smile faded as her brow creased in confusion. "We have strict visiting hours. You can't just waltz in here at any time and ask to see someone."

Gritting my teeth, I kept my smile in place. I didn't have time to abide by their rules. "Is Marv around?"

With an arched eyebrow, she studied me for a moment, then reached for the phone. A moment later, the sheriff emerged from the back.

"What's up, Tilly?" he asked, his eyes wide in surprise.

"I need to see Hank," I said. "Mama is so upset over this, and she's asked me to come down and talk to him."

Hopefully, his love for my mom would get me in the door.

"She could have come down herself," Marv said.

"Way too distraught," I replied with a shrug. "She can barely get out of bed and wanted me to check in on Hank."

I didn't bother with the truth—that she'd planned old Marv's murder in her mind dozens of times throughout the night.

"Well, I suppose I can make an exception," the sheriff said. "Not for you though… for Jennifer."

With a wide smile, I batted my eyelashes at him. "I appreciate that. It'll help put her mind at ease."

"Wait here a second," he said. "I'll be right back for you after I get him situated."

"Thank you."

Anything for Mama.

I stood and glanced around the small area, surprised by how similar it was to the sheriff's office in Oak Peak. Gray must be the uniform color of a sheriff's building across the nation.

A few moments later, Brewer returned. "Come on, Tilly. I'll give you ten minutes."

I followed him through the door and into a room to my right. Hank sat at the table dressed in an orange jumpsuit with cuffs on his wrists.

"Tilly!" he exclaimed with a smile as I walked in. "I'd give you a hug, but Marv says I've got to keep my caboose planted in this chair."

"It's okay," I said, blowing him a kiss. "Is everything okay?"

"Besides the fact my bed is about a foot too short for me, it's fine," Hank said, his tired eyes dancing with happiness. "I've got nothing to complain about."

"Ten minutes," Brewer said as he shut the door and I sat down.

"He obviously doesn't think I'm very dangerous or he'd never leave you in here with me," Hank whispered with a grin.

"You aren't dangerous," I said. "But we don't have much time. Did you hear from your lawyer?"

"Yes. I met with her first thing this morning. She's a strong woman, let me tell you. I'm glad she's on my side."

Derek had come through once again for me and my parents. How in the world did I get so lucky? "What did she say?"

"That I'll be out of here soon and she's going to eat Brewer's spleen for breakfast once she's done eviscerating him."

I chuckled and shook my head. "She sounds frightening."

"Like I said, I'm glad she's on my side."

"Hank, we need to talk about your knife."

The light mood we'd created vanished and a cloud of seriousness descended as his grin faded. "It's the darnedest thing. I can't remember where I lost it."

"You have to," I said. "It's the murder weapon, and

we need to know where someone found it. It may lead to finding the killer."

Biting his lip, he glanced around the room as if the answer could be found on the walls. "I just don't know, Tilly. It was a few days before you arrived. I can't remember what I had for lunch yesterday."

"Well, let's start with the morning you lost it and walk through the full day. What do you remember doing when you first woke up?"

He stared at the table for a long moment, then his cheeks turned crimson and he cleared his throat. "Well, your mama and I had marital relations before we got out of bed."

Ugh. That was the last thing I needed to hear, so I quickly moved the conversation along. "What then?"

Our gazes locked, and I could see that he was beginning to recall the day. "I went downstairs and made her some coffee, then I heated up some cinnamon rolls she'd bought at the bakery the day before. I put everything on a tray and brought it upstairs. We watched the news and had our coffee in bed."

"Okay, great. What happened next?"

"Well, I had to get the lawn mowed because they were going to deliver the tables and chairs in two days," he said, nodding. "Yes. I rode around the yard listening to some Beethoven on my Walkman. You know how I like to sing and pretend I'm conducting an orchestra." I grinned, having seen him out on the lawnmower singing at the top of his lungs many times. "I made sure I didn't miss any spots. I wanted your big day to be perfect."

"And it was," I said, appreciating his efforts. But a Walkman? I made a mental note to at least upgrade him to an iPod or show him how to download music on his phone.

"Your mama made me lunch," he said. "Is she doing okay? She's a tough cookie but this mess is a hard one to swallow."

"She's going to see Pastor Matthew today to get some help in cleansing her evil thoughts toward the sheriff."

Hank grinned and his eyes became teary. "That's my girl. I miss her already."

"Back to the knife," I said, the minutes ticking off in my head. "What happened after lunch?"

"Let's see... she made me a ham sandwich with a little too much mustard, but I'd never mention it to her. I had a boat tour that afternoon and..."

I stared at him expectantly, waiting for him to continue. His gaze flitted from the table to the wall behind me. "And what, Hank?"

"Well, I'll be a monkey's uncle," he whispered.

"Oh, my word," I muttered. "Tell me!"

"I had to feed Irwin," he said, grinning. "I took the knife down to the water to clean the fish to feed Irwin and I'd forgotten all about that. I left it by the water."

After hurrying out of the police station, I glanced around, unsure of what to do next. I should be going somewhere, doing something, but I had no idea what it should be. Instead, I walked across the street to the park and sat down. Green grass and trees stretched out in front of me as birds sang from above. Quiet and peaceful—just what I needed.

Hank had left his knife down by the water, which brought a whole new dimension to finding the killer.

I'd always assumed that the murderer had arrived by car, saw Kara, killed her, then motored on his or her way and no one had noticed in the melee.

But what if they'd arrived by boat, parked down

by the water, and made their way up the property, sight unseen? It wouldn't be hard. The area was heavily wooded and anyone could sneak around from tree to tree, especially when everyone had their attention focused on a wedding. Once Irwin had scared the living heck out of everyone and caused them to run for their lives, the killer could have moved in when Kara had been left alone. After doing the deed, he could have jaunted back to the water and taken off via boat. A ballsy plan, but definitely feasible.

However, he or she would need access to a boat. It seemed everyone in Louisiana had one, or knew of someone who did. But would a killer enlist another person to drive them to a place where they would commit murder, or would they arrive by themselves? I certainly wouldn't want anyone knowing my business it I was going to off someone, but maybe there were two people who wanted Kara dead?

The first thing I needed to do was find out who among my suspects had a boat.

I called Mama, who picked up after the second ring.

"What's up, Tilly?"

"Does Francois have a boat?" I asked.

"Yes, he does," she replied. "He loves going out on the water, especially for sunrise fishing."

"Okay, thanks."

I hung up and wondered about Cathy. She didn't strike me as the boating type, but neither did Francois. Besides, Francois was at my wedding. The timing didn't work for him to leave, get on his boat, and motor back over to my parents' house. From what Hank and Derek had claimed, Francois had left only a few minutes before the murder had taken place and I'd found the body. I supposed Francois needed to be crossed off my suspect list. Mama had been right.

The Russos... I knew next to nothing about them, except what the daughter's boyfriend, Mark, had shared with me and I'd heard through the grapevine. Certainly, if Mr. Russo had threatened Mark with taking him out to the Gulf of Mexico, chaining cement blocks to his feet and tossing him overboard, he had access to a boat. Or at the least, one of his goons did. I wasn't aware of the workings of the mob, except what I'd seen in movies and on television. But it would seem that the murder would be a perfect job for them. It required the cunning and stealth of a professional, something Cathy didn't have. Come to think of it, neither did Kara's boyfriend, Bubba, my last suspect. However, one thing I'd learned was I couldn't always take people at face value. Everyone had secrets to hide and often-times hid their true nature from the world.

The more I considered it, I definitely was looking for two different people: one who had done every-thing in their power to ruin my wedding, and the other who had killed Kara. There was no other explanation that made any sense.

Speaking of which... I needed to speak to George, Francois' employee who had told Kara to take the wrong truck and deliver the noodles to my wedding. I'd forgotten about him since he seemed the most harmless out of everyone. As far as I was aware, I'd never met the man, so why would he want to ruin my wedding?

Obviously, Kara's death was far more important than discovering who had sabotaged my big day, but maybe talking to George would help me glean more information on who had killed her.

I pulled out my phone again and called Francois.

"Tilly, love, how are you today?"

"I'm fine, Francois. And you?"

"Wonderful. I just booked a wedding for the fall. The bride is going to wear orange and the wedding will have a Halloween theme. I've been assured nothing too gory, but she's insisting that people wear black and all the decorations will be black and orange. It should be quite interesting."

"Huh," I said, trying to picture it. "What does she want for food?"

"We're going with a simple chicken dish and some sides, but for dessert, she was hoping I could create some eyeballs. Apparently, Halloween is her favorite time of year."

Despite my dire situation, I burst out laughing. "And I'm sure you can."

"Oh, yes. I'm actually making a batch right now to test my recipe. I'm quite excited by the originality of this one."

"It definitely sounds interesting," I said. "Take some pictures."

"Oh, I will. What can I do for you today?"

"Well, I was wondering if George was working and if I could stop by and see him."

"He'll be here in about an hour," Francois said. "What do you need him for?"

"I just wanted to ask him about the mistake on the food for my wedding," I said. "That's all."

Francois gave a ragged, overdrawn sigh. "I've been over that catastrophe with him already, but I suppose if you'd like to speak to him as well, then come on by. He's lucky he still has a job and that I have a forgiving heart."

"Speaking of forgiving hearts," I said, hoping to shift Francois' focus. "Sheriff Brewer arrested Hank last night for Kara's murder. Mama is with Pastor Matthew today because she's thought of fifty different ways she wants to kill Brewer and feels she needs help cleansing her evil thoughts."

"Oh, my word!" Francois exclaimed. "What has this world come to? What evidence does the sheriff have?"

"Apparently, Hank has a specially carved knife and it was the murder weapon."

A long silence stretched between us and I could practically hear Francois' brain churning through the information I'd given.

"I'm not certain how to explain that, but I'm sure Hank will be cleared," Francois finally stated. "He's a bit eccentric, but he's not a killer."

"Agreed," I said, standing. "I'm going to head over to your place now, if that's okay."

"Of course, Tilly. I look forward to seeing you, and you'll be just in time to eat a few eyeballs with me."

We both laughed again and I hung up, curious to see how the treats turned out.

As I strolled back to my rental car, the phone rang again. My heart skipped a beat when I read Carla, my friend in Oak Peak who was babysitting all my animals, calling.

"Hey!" I answered. "Is everything okay?"

"Yes," she said, but her voice revealed otherwise. "I wasn't sure whether to call you or not."

"What's going on? Did Tinker poo in the house? Did Belle get into a fight with your cat? Or did she jump on the counter and send a coffee cup flying? She can be so cranky sometimes. Or does one of them need to go to the vet? I can pay you back as soon as I get home. I'm so sorry, Carla. I know they miss—˜

"Tilly, stop. Just listen to me, okay?"

"All right," I said with a sigh. "What's going on?"

"Yes. Well, probably, but I'm not certain. Like I said, I wasn't sure if I should call you or not, but Mac thought I should."

Mac was Carla's husband and a great guy. Before I met Derek, I had wanted a relationship like they shared, and my prayers had been answered.

I slipped into my car and stared out the windshield, preparing myself for bad news. "Okay. I'm ready. Tell me."

"Tinker and Belle are fine. Tinker is definitely a

little depressed and Belle is becoming a bit crabbier, but I keep telling them you'll be home soon."

"And the chickens?"

"All is good there as well. Mac took Tinker over yesterday to feed them and she cheered up after spending some time with them."

I'd received the chickens as a gift, and although I'd never bonded with them, Tinker had. She loved spending time with them.

I closed my eyes in relief, but my heart ached with love for my two fur babies. I wanted to go home. "If they're okay, then what is it?"

"It's Byron."

My eyes flew open as confusion set in. Why would Carla think I cared one iota about Deputy Byron Mills? We'd dated briefly after my husband left me, and it hadn't worked out. I'd found him boring, but he'd never gotten over me. He'd been a Class A Jerk to Derek, and I wouldn't be sorry if I never saw him again. However, living in the small town of Oak Peak, I couldn't avoid him. "What about him?"

"Well, he went out of town for a few days."

"So?"

"He left the day before you went to Louisiana and said he was going fishing in Oregon."

"Well, I hope he had a great time," I replied. "What does this have to do with me?"

"I don't think he went to Oregon, Tilly. In fact, I'm sure of it."

"Where do you think he went?"

"Louisiana."

My breath hitched as I digested what Carla had said. "What makes you think that?"

"He came into the bakery late yesterday afternoon, claiming he was tired from his trip. We chatted for a few moments, then he sat down and had a cinnamon roll and some coffee. After he went back to work, I cleaned up his table where he'd left some receipts and stuff, like he'd emptied the garbage out of his wallet. I found an airline boarding pass from Louisiana to California."

Byron Mills had been in Louisiana? At the same time my wedding had gone to heck in a handbasket?

"When I think about all the stuff that went wrong at your wedding, I can't help but wonder if he was responsible," Carla continued. "I mean, there's no other reason for him to fly across the country for a few days, which happens to also be the place you're getting married."

I love you and I'll do everything in my power to make sure you don't marry that no good druggie.

Byron had said those exact words to me, but had he flown across the country to fulfill them?

"How would he know where my parents live?" I asked, still unable to believe he'd stoop to such levels.

"The internet, Tilly," Carla said. "Everything is on the internet if you know where to look for it."

My blood boiled so hot, I thought I may pass out. After starting the car, I blasted the air conditioner. "If you're right, Carla, I'm going to kill him. Dead. Deader than dead."

"Please try to calm down," she begged. "Please, Tilly. Being that upset isn't going to do you any good."

Perhaps I needed to join Mama in seeing Pastor Matthew to cleanse me of my wicked thoughts because I'd love nothing more than to stick a knife in the deputy's chest.

I had half a mind to call him right away and give him a tongue lashing he wouldn't forget, but I also told Francois I would be heading over. The drive would give me a chance to cool off and figure out how to gather evidence against Byron, because he'd never admit to any of it.

"Thanks for letting me know, Carla," I said, attempting to keep my voice even. "I appreciate you calling me."

"Tilly, you're scaring me," Carla said. "You're way too calm now."

"It's okay. I'm fine."

"Tilly, I hesitated to call because does any of it matter anymore? What's done is done, and do you really need the stress in your life right now? I don't want to see you going off the deep end and sharing a cell with Hank."

"I won't go off the deep end," I said. "But I will tell you this: Deputy Byron Mills is going to pay if he is the one responsible for screwing up my wedding. That, I promise you."

By the time I arrived at Francois' Fancy Foods, I had calmed down. Yes, my wedding at been ruined, possibly by Byron. The most important thing was to find the killer. Derek and I could have another wedding, but Kara would never have another life. On top of that, I wouldn't allow Hank to spend the rest of his years in jail for a crime he didn't commit. If Byron was responsible in any way, shape or form, I'd find out and deal with him at another time. He'd get his. I'd make sure of it.

Francois opened the door to the converted warehouse and waved as I parked my car. I smiled and took a deep breath before exiting, then grinned at my reflection in the rearview mirror. Just because I wanted to rip someone's head off didn't mean I couldn't be polite to others who weren't involved.

"Tilly! Just in time for some eyeballs!"

We laughed as he hugged me, my cheek brushing against his gray wool suit. "Come into my den of deliciousness."

I noted the vans with the business name parked to my left. Inside, I followed Francois through a small waiting area furnished with overstuffed yellow couches and purple walls and into a large professional kitchen stocked with shiny appliances and wonderful smells.

"The eyeballs literally just came out of the oven," Francois said. "Please, join me."

I glanced at the orbs staring back at me from the baking sheet. Some were blue, others green or brown. None looked overly-appetizing.

"Why are they different colors?" I asked.

"Well, people have different colored eyes."

I studied them a little closer. "They look real, Francois."

"Excellent! The blue is blueberry, the green is mint, and the brown is chocolate. I was thinking I'd add a strawberry and possibly a licorice flavor as well. Will you please try one?"

"Do I have to? They're a little too realistic for me."

"Of course you don't have to, but it would be appreciated. I need feedback on the taste."

Well, he had allowed me into his inner sanctuary to talk to George. The least I could do is eat an eyeball.

I picked the blue and shoved it into my mouth. The rush of blueberry flavor exploded over my taste-buds and I moaned in delight. "These are so good!"

"Oh, excellent!" he exclaimed as he picked up a brown one and took a bite. "I think the chocolate needs some work."

Next, I chose a mint. It wasn't my favorite flavoring, but I still nodded in approval. "I like this, but it can't compare to the blueberry."

"Wonderful," Francois said. "Thank you for being my guinea pig."

"My pleasure. I wasn't sure I would enjoy that, but you're one heck of a baker."

"Thank you, Tilly," he said, his voice sincere with appreciation. "It means so much to me, especially after your wedding debacle."

"Yeah, that was awful," I said. "The killer needs to be found."

"Do you really think George can help with that?"

"I doubt it," I said with a sigh. "But he was

involved with the wedding, so I feel like I should speak to him."

"Agreed. Let me fetch him for you, okay? You two can talk in my office."

I followed Francois out of the kitchen to a small room containing a tidy desk stacked with piles of perfectly papers. "If you could, *s'il vous plaît*, don't touch anything. I'm very particular about my paper-work system to keep myself organized."

"Of course."

After sitting in a yellow chair, I wished I had a glass of water. The sugar had settled in my mouth and I would have liked to wash it down.

"And Tilly, if you think George is responsible for Kara's death, I want to know about it immediately. I don't see how he could be, but please keep me informed."

I gave him a thumbs up and he left, returning a moment later with his employee.

In his thirties, or maybe forties, he gave off a good-old-boy vibe with his jeans, belt buckle, and cowboy boots. Standing next to Francois dressed impeccably in his wool suit, I wondered if I'd ever seen two people so mismatched. Frankly, I was surprised George worked for Francois.

"George, this is Tilly. Tilly, this is George. You two have a lovely conversation."

Francois hurried off, leaving us alone.

"Hey," George offered, stuffing his hands in his front pockets.

"Hello. Thank you for meeting with me. Do you want to have a seat?"

"Sure."

George sat across from me. "Are you the cops or something?"

I shook my head, surprised Francois hadn't informed him I was coming. "My name's Tilly Bordeaux. I'm the one who had the mix up and received noodles at my wedding instead of Creole food."

His eyes widened and he shook his head. "Aw, man. I never would have agreed to talk to you if I had known."

"How come?" I asked.

"Because... because I feel bad about what happened."

I couldn't shake the feeling that he was hiding something or there was a lot more to the story than he was letting on. "Thank you," I said quietly.

"You know, don't you? I can tell by the way you're looking at me. You know."

Nodding slowly, I wondered what information I supposedly had.

"Aww man. I'm sorry for what I did."

Was he sorry for the truck mix-up which resulted in the noodles at my wedding, or something more?

"Please tell me everything," I said. "It's really important for me to understand."

George rubbed his face and glanced around the room, as if he weren't sure where to begin. "My wife is pregnant and we need the money."

"Go on."

My heart thumped double time as I realized I could finally be getting some answers to what happened.

"The guy said you were making a mistake by getting married. In fact, he wondered if you had been forced into it, or that you weren't in your right frame of mind."

I was pretty certain of the answer, but I had to hear it for myself. "Did that guy have a name?"

"He said his name was Smith, but I thought he was lying. Huge guy, looks like he works out a lot. Didn't tell me his first name."

There was only one man who looked like he worked out a lot that would say I was making a mistake by wedding Derek. "Tell me what else he said."

"He wanted to ruin your wedding and paid me to do it."

And there it was. I sat back in my chair and stared at the nervous man in front of me. He'd taken payment from Byron to destroy my big day. "How much?"

"Three hundred."

For five months, I'd been carrying around a laptop that had all our wedding plans. I'd talked about them at length at Debbie's Deliciousness. Byron could have easily overheard a dozen times that Francois' Fancy Food Catering would be supplying the meal.

I nodded and sighed. "A lot of things went wrong that day, George. Can you tell me exactly what you were responsible for? Was it anything but the food?"

He wouldn't look at me, but instead kept his gaze on the floor. "The food, I cut the speaker wire... he told me there was a gator on property and I put some fish around to try to get the gator to interrupt the party."

"It worked wonderfully," I said. "Now tell me this: did you cause the pastor to have a car accident?"

"Of course not!" he said. "I wouldn't physically hurt anyone!"

He obviously couldn't make it rain, either.

"So the speaker wire, the gator, and the food mix-up were all thanks to you," I said.

"Wait. I thought you knew all that?"

"I had an idea," I said, standing. Liar, liar pants on fire once again. "But thanks for the confirmation. Tell me when you cut the wire."

"It was the night before the ceremony," he said, his voice meek. "I set the fish out and sliced the wire then. I found the gator down by the water, but he didn't move when he saw me. I didn't think he was going to follow my trail, but I set them out anyway."

Hank had fed Irwin a few days before we arrived, thinking he'd stay by the shore while his food digested. I guess Irwin couldn't resist a bass lying under a tree. He most likely had also been curious about what was going on in his backyard. Irwin may have shown up during the wedding with or without the fish luring him, but only Irwin could answer that, and he wasn't the chatty type.

"And how did you get onto the property?" I asked.

"By the water," he mumbled. "Just pulled my boat right up there."

"And did you see anything or anyone else who looked suspicious?"

George shook his head. "It was the middle of the night. No one was around but me."

Beyond exhausted, I couldn't even rally myself to be angry at George. At least I knew that Kara's murder was a totally separate issue.

"You did all that for three hundred bucks, huh?" I asked shaking my head. "You should be ashamed of yourself."

"I am," George replied, his shoulder slumping. "We need the money—my wife is pregnant! That guy said I'd be doing you a favor, and that's how I justified it."

"Well, he was wrong," I said as I exited the office.

"I'm sorry!" George yelled after me as I walked down the hall.

Giving him a wave over my shoulder, I called, "Good luck with the baby!"

Desperate people do desperate things.

Byron had thrown one last hail Mary to stop me from marrying Derek, and he'd certainly gone above and beyond in his quest. There was something wrong with that man. His deck was short a few spades.

I found Francois in the entryway sitting on his

yellow couch reading the paper and sipping a cup of tea. With a grin, he set it down when he saw me.

"Did it go okay?" he asked.

"Yes," I said with a sigh as I sat down next to him. "George was responsible for a lot of the things that went wrong at my wedding, but he didn't kill Kara."

Francois nodded. "That food mix-up was planned then, and not a mistake as he originally told me?"

"Yep." I also listed George's other sins.

"I need to fire him."

"Please don't," I said, laying my hand on his forearm. "He's got a baby on the way and he needs the money."

Francois glanced over at me with an arched eyebrow. "You're very kind, Tilly. But I can't trust him anymore."

"I think you can. He feels awful for what he did and needs this job. Besides, he was acting out of desperation and doing what someone was paying him to do... Somehow he convinced himself it was the right thing. If he loses his job, I'm afraid he'll try to rob a bank or something."

"Very well," Francois said with a long sigh. "However, he's on probation. One more *faux pas*, and he shall find himself in the unemployment line."

"That's fair," I said. "I think he'll be on his best behavior, though. "

"I'll have a discussion with him."

Leaning forward, I picked up the paper Francois had been reading, happy that people still received the physical product. "Anything interesting?"

"Actually, yes," Francois said. "Turn to page three."

The headline immediately caught my eye: *Groom Goes Missing*

On day two of their honeymoon in Turks and Caicos, Mark Setzer woke early to go for a run on the beach. He never returned.

"It's like he disappeared into thin air," Nicola Setzer told this reporter. "Something happened to him and the authorities don't know what."

Nicola Setzer, formerly Nicola Russo, returned from the Caribbean after spending three days searching for her groom. The Turks and Caicos authorities continue their hunt for the missing man.

"Oh, my word," I whispered.

"Do you think Russo got him?" Francois asked.

I shook my head. "When I went to see Nicola, I met Mark. He said he had to run away from her and her crazy family. I got the impression he was going to try to do so on the honeymoon."

"Really? How interesting."

"That's just between you and me."

"Of course."

I scanned the rest of the article, imagining Mark living in the rainforest of the island. Or maybe he'd jumped on a boat to any of the other seven thousand islands in the Caribbean. Whatever he'd done, I wished him well.

"I better get back to my parents' house," I said, standing. "At least I know who ruined my wedding."

"Yes. And I hope the authorities will find the real killer."

"Me too," I replied, not at all hopeful.

That would be up to me.

CHAPTER 18

When I arrived back at my parents' house, I found Debbie sitting in the living room alone staring at her phone.

"Where is everyone?" I asked, plopping down on the couch next to her, noting she had been playing Candy Crush. Fitting for a baker.

"Derek went to go visit Hank in the slammer; your mom wrote a note saying she was going to visit Pastor Matthew. But the million-dollar question is, where have you been?"

"I was gone right after the sun came up."

"Figures. Where did you run off to, leaving me all by my poor lonesome, to fend for myself?"

"Oh, come on," I chided. "You're a big girl. I went to Francois' Fancy Food Catering."

"What did you do there?"

"I ate eyeballs and talked to George."

"Eyeballs?"

Nodding, I turned to my friend. "You need to go there and ask him for the recipe. They would either be a huge hit in Oak Peak, or you'd be run out of town."

I explained the dessert and her eyes lit up. "Oh, I can't wait to make those and see what people think. I'll probably be dragged down to the church for an exorcism."

"Probably. But honestly, they were delicious, the blueberry being my favorite."

"Tell me about the rest of your visit."

On the way home, I had decided I wouldn't reveal Byron's interference with the wedding. George had cut the speaker wire, lured Irwin up to the ceremony, and played around with the food order. The rain still would have come and the pastor wouldn't have shown. He had helped to ruin the wedding, but the day still wouldn't have been the perfect ceremony we'd all imagined if he hadn't accepted Byron's offer.

"Well, I was just talking with Francois about Kara's murder."

"What did he have to say?"

"Whoever killed her had to come from the water because that's where Hank lost his knife. So, it has to be someone who has access to a boat."

"We're in Louisiana. Isn't that everyone?"

"Just about."

"Francois also showed me an article about the noodle bride. Her husband has gone missing."

Debbie gasped, her eyes glazing over like when she heard some incredible secret. "No kidding!"

"Yes. They were on their honeymoon on one of those fancy islands in the Caribbean and he got up early to go for a run. She hasn't seen him since."

"His father-in-law did him in. That's my guess on who killed Kara," Debbie said, nodding her head. "The crazy mob guy, Russo."

"Why do you think that?"

"If he offed his daughter's husband, then why wouldn't he get revenge on Francois for the food mix up by killing his employee?"

"Too extreme," I said, doubtfully. "I don't think he killed the groom. Mark told me he was going to bolt."

"Even if that were the truth, you are dealing with the mob."

"But the dad is supposed to live a quiet life," I argued. "He *ratted* on the mob. He's not going to do something that may splash his face all over the news and put a target on his chest."

"Yes, but his daughter's *wedding* was ruined. Whoever was working his wedding would know exactly where the other truck was located. And who's to say he did nothing but tell someone else to get revenge for him?"

"You do have a point."

"Of course I do. He threatened to throw an innocent man overboard with cement blocks for breaking up with his cheating daughter. The guy is nuts, Tilly. Certifiable."

"Let's say you're right," I replied. "How do we go about proving he's the murderer?"

"I don't know," Debbie said, shrugging. "You're the super sleuth. I'm just along for the ride and to provide my theories."

We could get the address from Francois and go interview the man. He wouldn't want to chat with a reporter. Perhaps tell him we were friends of Nicola's?

"What about the eyeball creator, Francois?" Debbie asked. "He was furious. I could easily see him knifing Kara for the mistake."

"Really? He seems so harmless."

"He's a perfectionist, like me," Debbie said. "I've

thought about stabbing a few of my short-lived employees who messed things up."

"You have not!"

"Well, I'd never follow through, but I've thought about it."

"The mistake would have to be something pretty serious in order for you to go that far," I said.

"True, but Kara brought the wrong food to a wedding. It's a direct reflection of Francois' business, and if I were him, it would make me furious."

"George told her what truck to take."

"She should have verified it by looking inside and inspecting the food," Debbie said. "Mistakes can be avoided if everyone double-checks everyone else."

Debbie had a point, and I wondered why Kara never did double-check the order her van carried, but I'd never know.

"If he *is* guilty, I don't want him arrested until he teaches me how to make those eyeballs," Debbie said.

I rolled my eyes and shook my head. "Of course. Why would I want my stepfather out of jail before you learned to make a dessert?" We both laughed. "Besides, I don't think the timing works with Francois being the killer. The best I can tell, the time of the murder is after Francois left to head over to the Russo wedding."

"So that leaves us with Hank and Bubba," Debbie said with a sigh. "And we know Hank didn't do it."

"In order for Bubba to have killed Kara, he'd have needed a boat."

"He said he was hurt in a fishing accident, so my guess is he's got one." Debbie said. "Remember his limp? Once a rodman, always a rodman."

"But it doesn't mean he killed Kara."

"What are you talking about?" Debbie asked, shooting to her feet. "He practically admitted it!"

Thinking back to the conversation, she was once again correct. *If I couldn't have her, no one should.* "Well, let's say you're right. How do we prove it?"

"I don't know," Debbie said, beginning to pace. "I guess we go and see him again. It's not like he's overly busy or anything. We can catch him in between twelve-packs."

I grimaced just thinking about stepping foot in Bubba's apartment again, and frustration welled within me. No matter how many times we talked about the suspects, nothing stood out, leading me to believe in their guilt.

"Have you looked to see who owns a boat through public records?" Debbie asked.

She should have slapped me. I'd have been less

stunned. "No," I said through gritted teeth. "It never even occurred to me."

"Good thing you've got me around," Debbie said, chuckling. "Go get your computer."

I hurried to the second floor and grabbed my laptop off the bed, then ran back down the stairs. If Mama had been home, she would have made a comment about a herd of antelope and asked me to tread quietly.

After sitting down next to Debbie, I opened my laptop. "Francois has a boat," I said. "Mama confirmed that. He enjoys fishing."

"Okay, so we can't cross him off the list. In fact, he moves to the top."

"I think you're barking up the wrong tree on that one," I muttered. "The timing doesn't match up right."

"Arf, arf. We'll see about that."

I navigated to the public records and typed in *Russo.*

"Well, looky there," Debbie said. "Nicola Russo has a boat. I don't see anything about a man with that last name owning one."

"Me neither," I said. "We now know Russo definitely had access to one. I wonder where it's kept?"

"I don't know much about boats except that

owning one is like flushing dollar bills down the toilet. My guess is it's either in dry storage somewhere, or at a marina. Unless he's got it up on a trailer in his front drive, but for some reason that doesn't scream rich mob guy to me. More weekend fisherman."

"There was a small marina by Nicola's apartment!" I exclaimed.

"Where was her wedding?"

" I never asked. Let's call Francois."

A moment later, we had our answer, and my hands trembled with excitement. "They held it at a country club about two miles away from the marina."

"Easy and quick access to the boat," Debbie said, rubbing her hands together, a huge grin on her face. "Search for Cathy. From what you've told me, she's a piece of work."

"Half-crazy, I swear it." I typed in her name and scanned my screen. "Nothing on owning a boat." A dead end. But, oh... maybe not.

"What is it?" Debbie asked as I held my cursor over a link. When I clicked it, I received more information than I bargained for.

"Cathy doesn't own a boat, but she does have a criminal record."

"Oh, my word. For what?"

"Assault."

"On who?"

"Hang on." I quickly read through the report. "A bride in Georgia who left her a bad review online."

Debbie gasped. "Are you kidding me?"

I shook my head. "Nope. Cathy tried to run the woman over in a parking lot."

"Unbelievable. If she were guilty, I don't see it as too far of a jump between that and ruining a competitor's wedding and killing one of his employees for good measure."

With a sigh, I rubbed the bridge of my nose.

"So, no boat, but attempted murder," Debbie said. "Filing that away for future reference. Check out our old friend, Bubba."

I typed in his name and found nothing, which disappointed me because I thought out of all the suspects, he'd be the one.

"Not having a boat registered means nothing," Debbie said. "He could have a friend who owns a boat and he used it to kill Kara."

"He did have our address. Kara's planner was sitting out on the counter in the kitchen."

"Well, this search has given us nothing but more

confusion," Debbie said, letting her head fall back against the cushions. "Dang it all."

My friend was tired, and I didn't blame her. She'd been sitting idle for almost a full week past the wedding. Debbie usually ran full throttle. It energized her, and the waiting was slowly draining her. Besides, she needed to get back to her business.

"Why don't you make reservations to go home?" I suggested yet again. "They've arrested Hank. You can leave now. The sheriff has no interest in you."

She shook her head. "I'm not going anywhere until you and Derek go with me, Tilly. So, use that noggin and figure out who killed Kara."

Turning back to my computer screen, I stared at it a long time. Debbie was right. Our search hadn't added any great clues to the investigation. Yet, I couldn't stop thinking about Cathy and Bubba—they'd both been a little psycho and I figured we should probably start with them, even though neither had a boat. The thought of approaching the Russos scared me to death, and I knew in my heart Francois hadn't stabbed Kara. The timeline really didn't work out for him.

Cathy or Bubba made more sense. But so did Russo, yet I didn't have the courage to approach him.

"I think we should really investigate Cathy and

Bubba," I said. "And if we can't prove anything with either one, then we'll tell the police about them all and have them speak to Russo."

"Sounds good," Debbie replied. "I like a solid plan. Who do you want to start with?"

"Bubba," I said. "Let's go see Bubba."

"And why did you choose him?"

"I have no idea," I replied. "Just a gut feeling talking to Bubba is the right way to go for now."

CHAPTER 19

"Was that Bubba?" Debbie asked on our way over to his apartment. I glanced in the rearview mirror to see an old white pickup truck.

"I didn't notice."

Debbie turned and looked out the back window. "I'm right around ninety percent sure that's him. Flip a U-turn and let's follow him."

After doing as instructed, I sped up to catch him. Once I had him firmly in my sight, I slowed a little and let one car in the lane between us.

"This is what they do in the cop shows," Debbie said. "Good thinking, Tilly."

"Thanks."

We trailed him for a few more minutes, then I asked, "Where do you think he's going?"

"Beats me. We'll find out sooner or later."

When he moved over to the left-hand turn lane, I debated following since I'd be right behind him. I passed him and continued on my way.

"Go back!" Debbie yelled. "Go back or we're going to lose him!"

"I will," I said, switching lanes. "I just didn't want to be on his tail."

After making a left into a parking lot, I merged back on to the main road and then turned right where Bubba had gone. I hadn't noted the sign at the entrance, but it became clear to me that we had arrived at a dry storage for boats.

"Isn't this interesting," Debbie said. "We were just talking about boats."

I slowly drove through the rows that stood three vessels high on each side, looking for the white pickup.

"This place is huge," Debbie muttered. "We may have lost him."

On the next aisle, a forklift blocked our way as it raised its arms to the top shelf and slowly pulled out a boat.

"That's pretty amazing," Debbie said. "I'd be terrified I'd drop the dang thing."

"Me, too."

Once he cleared the path, we continued our search.

"He may be gone by now," Debbie grumbled. "We should have followed him in."

"Don't be such a downer," I replied. "We'll find him."

Five minutes later, we rounded a corner and I caught a glimpse of the pickup at the end of the aisle.

"There's the truck," I whispered, quickly throwing the rental car in reverse and whipping back around the way I'd come.

"What are you doing?"

"We'll head that way down this aisle on foot. He'll never see us."

"Good thinking."

We exited the car and trotted as quietly as possible toward the truck, keeping one row of boats between us and our target.

"Shh," I whispered when I heard voices as we approached. I grabbed Debbie's arm and we stopped. "Listen."

Two men, but we weren't close enough for me to

understand their conversation. It came across more as two deep rumbles of noise.

"Let's move closer," Debbie murmured. "I can't make out what they're saying."

I nodded and we slowly made our way, the rocks under our shoes seeming so loud, I was certain the sound would alert the pair to our arrival.

We crouched down when they stood directly on the other side.

"There it is," Bubba said, then let out a long burp.

"Yes. I can see that."

Debbie glanced over at me, her brow knitted in a frown. "Is that Francois?" she mouthed.

I nodded, also bewildered by his presence.

"You're aware there are laws against drinking beer while operating a motor vehicle, correct?" Francois asked.

The sound of a can being crushed filled the air. "Don't lecture me, you hoity-toity jerk. Kara always said she liked you, and I couldn't figure out why."

"Maybe because she had some taste," Francois said, barely loud enough for us to hear, but Debbie snickered.

"What does that mean?" Bubba asked. The poor guy really was stupid.

"Nothing, nothing," Francois replied, then sighed. "I'm just not sure what to do with the boat."

Was it Francois' boat? The records had shown that Bubba didn't own one. And if it did belong to Francois, what was he doing with it? The whole meeting seemed confusing and shady to me.

"How about you just give me the money you owe?" Bubba said, popping another can open.

Wait. Francois owed Bubba money? For what? Francois had been pretty clear he didn't think much of Bubba, so I didn't understand why they were meeting and what the man would be paying him for.

"She would have wanted this," Bubba continued.

Francois chuckled. "Don't use your dead girl-friend like that, Bubba. It's very unbecoming of you."

"Well, she would have."

"Let me ask you this," Francois said. "Did you kill her?"

"Of course not!" Bubba yelled, sounding pretty convincing. "I loved her! I needed her! Why would I do that?"

Francois began to pace, coming in and out of my line of sight. He crossed his arms over his chest and stared down Bubba. "You are a sorry excuse for a man, especially for a woman like Kara."

"I don't need to sit here and listen to you insult

me," Bubba said, throwing a beer can at Francois. "Just give me my money!"

"We're never going to figure out what happened," Debbie whispered. "We need to confront them both."

Before I answered, Bubba charged Francois and both tumbled to the ground. Bubba straddled Francois, who yelled about his ruined suit.

"Pay me my money!" Bubba screamed.

"Get off me, you brute! You're destroying the wool!"

How he could wear such heavy material in the heat, I'd never understand. But as Bubba raised his fist and slammed it into Francois' face, I realized we had a big problem. "Call the police, Debbie. Once you've done that, come help me." I ran around the row of boats, not waiting for an answer. "Stop it! Stop it, Bubba!"

The man turned to me, his fist raised once again. His stare bore into me as if he couldn't quite place where he'd seen me before. Then his arms slowly lowered to his side, and Francois pushed him off. Both sat on the ground breathing hard, but glaring at me as if I'd ruined a party.

"What's going on here?" I asked.

"What are you doing here?" Francois asked, staggering to his feet as he wiped down his suit with his palms.

"Who are you again?" Bubba asked.

"My name's Tilly Bordeaux," I said. "I met you a few days ago."

"Oh, right. Condolences and stuff on Kara."

"Correct," I said, keeping my eye on both, unsure who I should trust.

"Whose boat is this?" I asked, pointing at the vessel they'd been speaking of.

"It's about to be his," Bubba said. "He wants to buy it off me."

Francois narrowed his gaze at the man. "I *never* insinuated that. What I *did* say is that I would consider it, based on my love for Kara, but what I had to figure out is if she'd *want* me to do so or instead, have you drown in your own sorry state of fraud, drunkenness, and laziness."

"I ain't no fraud!" Bubba yelled as he scrambled to his feet and took a few steps toward Francois again. I questioned my own sanity when I stepped between them, but I noted he didn't fight Francois on the drunkenness or laziness accusations.

"Knock it off!" I shouted, hoping I sounded forceful enough Bubba would calm down. "What happened here?" Turning to Francois, I asked, "Why does he want you to buy the boat?"

Francois sighed and straightened his lapel. Despite just being hit, he seemed unfazed and more worried about the state of his suit. "He called me and asked me to meet him here to buy Kara's boat to help him out financially. I am trying to decide whether to do so or not, but this man is an absolute neanderthal so I'm thinking my answer is a hard no!"

"You *need* to buy the boat!" Bubba screamed. "You said you would!"

I narrowed my gaze at Bubba. This sale seemed far too important. I turned and studied the vessel. Nothing special about it at all. Perhaps it had been kept for weekend use, but it didn't venture into deep waters. "Kara owned this?"

Bubba nodded. "Yes. My love owned it, and she'd want Franky here to help me by buying it."

"Francois! My name is not Franky, but Francois! *Cochon!*"

"Whatever," Bubba mumbled.

"Have you put it up for sale?" I asked, wishing we'd searched for Kara owning a boat. "Put up signs around the marina or something?"

Bubba stared at me a moment as if I'd just asked

him if he'd spoken to the resident aliens visiting from Mars. "No."

"Why not?"

"Because I want Francois to buy it!" he yelled, and I knew something was off. He acted as if his life depended on Francois handing over cash for the boat. Why not get the money from somewhere else?

Glancing up at the vessel, I realized I could climb the rack and easily hop in. "I may buy it," I said. "Can I look around inside?"

"No!" Bubba said. "It's Francois' boat! He just needs to pay me!" Out of the corner of my eye, I noted he'd pulled out a gun. He must have been storing it in the back of his jeans. "Pay me!"

Something was on the boat that he didn't want anyone to see. I raised my hands to my shoulders and stepped slowly backward, toward the vessel. "You don't need use that, Bubba," I said as he swung it toward me.

"Give me the money or I'll shoot her!" he yelled at Francois.

With my heart thundering and sweat trickling down my face, I glanced at where Debbie should be hiding and saw nothing to indicate she was still there. Had she run away after calling the police?

"Okay, Bubba," Francois said, his voice smooth

and silky, as if he dealt with gun wielding drunks every day. "I'll retrieve the money from my car. It's parked right in front of yours over there. Just please, put the weapon down."

"Go get it!" Bubba screamed. He held the gun on me, while tilting the beer can to his mouth with his other hand.

Francois slowly walked toward his car, opened the door, and slipped inside. It looked as if he was messing with something on the front passenger seat, but I couldn't tell exactly what he was doing.

The cops should be on their way, but I didn't hear any sirens. And where in the world had Debbie gone?

"Just give me my money," Bubba muttered, swaying where he stood. "I need the money."

Out of the corner of my eye, I spotted Debbie approaching, pulling a blonde woman by the hair behind her, and finally, sirens wailed in the distance.

"Check that boat!" Debbie yelled. "Something is in that boat!"

I ran around the back of said boat just when Bubba started firing at me, and I screamed as I crouched behind it, praying he was a terrible shot. I slithered over the side like a snake and crawled along the floor. Pulling everything from every nook and cranny I could find, I searched for something—anything that could give me a clue to the truth.

"Let go of me!" someone yelled, and I could only guess it was whoever Debbie had captured.

"Put the gun down, Bubba!" Debbie shouted. Meanwhile, the sirens grew closer. "The cops are almost here, and you're done for! Don't make everything worse for yourself than it already is!"

With the boat being so small, I was running out of places to look for... what? I had no idea. I heard the clanking of metal hitting the gravel, which I assumed was the gun, so I took the chance to stand up just a bit and open the engine cover. At first, I didn't see it because it had been stuck behind the engine. When I pulled it out, I realized it was a T-shirt with bloodstains.

Leaving it there, I jumped down to the gravel and saw Debbie had Cathy from Cathy's Catering by the hair, and she'd also confiscated Bubba's gun. He sat on the ground at her feet.

"Umm... good work?" I said, unsure of what it all meant.

"Tell us what's going on here, Bubba," Debbie said, nudging him in the back with her knee while Cathy squirmed to get away. Debbie turned the gun on her. "And if you don't knock it off and sit your butt down, I'll put a bullet in your foot. Don't test my patience, woman."

Cathy sank to the ground next to Bubba while Francois emerged from his car, his arms crossed over his chest, his face pinched in confusion.

"What did you find in that boat?" Debbie asked.

I glanced at Bubba and Cathy, trying to make the pieces fit together, but I was at a loss. "A bloody shirt."

CHAPTER 20

Sheriff Brewer rolled up and emerged with his gun drawn. Debbie lifted her arms in the air and dropped the weapon when he ordered her to do so.

"What the heck is going on here?" Brewer demanded a moment later. "Someone better explain this to me and do it quickly before I take all of you in!"

"There's a bloody shirt in the boat," I said. "And it belongs to Kara Lionheart."

"The boat or the shirt?" Brewer asked.

"The boat."

"So what?" Brewer yelled.

"So, we haven't figured anything out yet!" I

shouted back. I turned to Francois, waiting for an explanation.

He rolled his eyes and shook his head, then cleared his throat as if he were going to give an important speech. "Bubba called me and asked me here to buy Kara's boat. He said it would help him greatly, and being how much I'd loved her, I wanted to do something to assist him. That's all I know. The rest of this is a puzzle to me as well."

"Why are you here, Cathy?" I asked. "And where did you find her, Debbie?"

"She arrived shortly after we did," Debbie replied. "I saw her sneaking around and I grabbed her."

"Why are you here, Cathy?" Brewer asked, repeating my question.

Shaking her head, she refused to answer and stared at the ground.

"She's here to make sure Francois buys the boat," Bubba said, then burst into tears. "Kara. I miss you."

Bubba was very drunk, and I felt more stumped than ever. Judging by the looks of puzzlement I noted on everyone's face, no one else had a clue, either. I approached him slowly and dropped to my haunches in front of him. The smell of beer and body odor engulfed me and my stomach churned at the odor, as well as what remained of my fear from being shot at. It seemed the man was ready to confess and explain everything. "Bubba, why is there a bloody shirt in Kara's boat?"

"Because I killed her," he said, sobbing. "I killed my Kara. That's my shirt."

"And why is Cathy here?" I asked gently.

"Don't you answer that, you pathetic idiot!" Cathy yelled.

"Shut it, lady," Debbie muttered. "We're finally going to get to the bottom of this."

Bubba looked at Cathy, then at me. "Cathy asked Kara to help take down Francois' business. Kara refused."

"Okay," I said, nodding. "What happened to Kara?"

"I had to kill her," Bubba sobbed. "She was going to leave me. No one but me could have my Kara."

The man cried uncontrollably, but I was still confused about how Cathy fit into the whole story.

"Why am I here?" Francois asked, his hands fisted at his sides. "What is *she* doing here?" He pointed at Cathy.

"Whatever is going on here, the jig is up," Brewer said. "Start talking, Cathy."

Her jaw worked as she stared down Francois

with absolute disdain in her gaze. "I wanted him ruined once and for all."

"And how exactly did you plan to do that?" Francois asked.

"I've been following your catering trucks to weddings for a while now," Cathy said. "To observe and see what I can do better."

More like what she could do to sabotage him.

Francois lifted his chin and smiled. "Well, that's smart. If you want to learn, you should study the best."

"When I followed Kara that day, it became apparent the wedding was a complete disaster," Cathy continued. "I almost left, but then I saw old Bubba here stab her as she was getting into the van at the gate, then he disappeared back onto the property."

Bubba did have access to a boat—Kara's boat. He also knew exactly where she was going to be that day because she'd written my parents' address in her planner. A quick internet search would bring up pictures of the house and show the water access.

"Why did you choose to kill her at my wedding?" I asked.

"I needed a place that would give the police a lot

of other suspects," Bubba said. "If I did it at home, I'd be the only one the police would look at."

"Tell me about that day," I said, glancing over at Brewer. His face had paled, but he listened intently.

"I pulled up the boat to the property, and I could see everyone sitting down," he said. "No one seemed to notice me, so I got out and found a knife lying there. I took it as a sign that I needed to kill Kara with it."

"You found a knife and suddenly it's a sign you need to murder your girlfriend?" Debbie asked.

Bubba nodded. "I wasn't sure how I was going to do it. Maybe mess with the brakes on the van. Or choke her. I didn't know. The knife would be quick and easy, so I walked up through the trees. Ran into a gator. I'm not sure who was more scared: him or me. He took off for the ceremony and all heck broke loose."

People had been scurrying around and screaming trying to escape Irwin, who had apparently been frightened by his run in with Bubba. No one had noticed the man in the total chaos.

"I hid in the trees and waited until everyone was gone except Kara. Then I killed her and walked back down to the water the way I'd come. That's my bloody shirt in the boat," he blurted in between sobs.

"Then you told Bubba you knew about the murder," I said, glancing over at Cathy.

"I had a plan—a good one—to take down Francois once and for all," Cathy muttered through gritted teeth.

"How were you going to do that?" Debbie asked.

"I told Bubba to hide his bloody shirt in Kara's boat, come up with some sob story about how he needed the money, and sell it to Francois. Then, once it was in Francois' name, I'd make an anonymous call to the cops and tell them where to find the shirt with Kara's blood all over it. He'd go down for the murder."

Debbie gasped and I stared at the crazy woman. I had to admit, her plan was solid. Sneaky, but very solid. Forensics on the shirt may eventually clear Francois, but he'd be out of commission for a long time until that happened. If we hadn't followed Bubba to the boat storage, Francois could have been sitting in prison very soon.

"How dare you!" Francois shouted. "How dare you try to ruin my good name. I could have gone to prison!"

"That was the point," Cathy yelled. "You'd be out of my hair and I'd be the number one caterer in this area!"

Francois walked over and leaned over Cathy, shaking his finger in her face. "You can't get rid of me that easily, Cathy. And if you wanted to be number one, you only need to serve food that is better than mine, not stuff I wouldn't feed my dog… if I actually owned one of those beasts."

I turned to Sheriff Brewer and our gazes locked. He cleared his throat as he strolled over with two pairs of handcuffs.

"When will Hank be set free?" I asked.

"I'll have him home by tonight."

"Make it by four and we won't sue you," I said.

Pulling Francois to the side, I could see his face was still pinched in anger, but his features softened when I spoke.

"Do you think we can do it?" I asked after I'd finished laying out my plan.

"*Absolument!*" he exclaimed. "Oh, this is exciting. I'm thrilled to be a part of it. I must go as I have work to do."

"We'll see you later!" I called as he hurried back to his car.

MY WEDDING WAS nothing like I had planned, but it turned out perfect.

Sheriff Brewer drove Hank home himself and delivered him a half-hour early. Although my stepdad was tired, he perked up after a swig from his flask while I told everyone what I intended to do.

"This is fantastic," Derek said, drawing me into an embrace and squeezing tight. "I can't wait to marry you, to make it official."

Mama and Debbie popped open a bottle of champagne just as Francois arrived. We never got the Creole feast I had originally wanted, but he did bring Chinese takeout along with some blueberry eyeballs.

Derek and I were married at sunset in my parents' backyard with Irwin lounging in his tub. A light breeze wafted off the water, causing the trees to gently sway. I wore my pajamas and Derek opted for a pair of sweatpants, a T-shirt, and his bow tie from his tuxedo. Debbie read the traditional vows from her phone, but Derek interrupted her when she got to the part about me obeying him.

"Can we do that line again?" he asked. "Tilly is her own person and does as she pleases, and that's one of the many reasons I love her. I don't want her to make a promise to me that I know she can't keep."

And so, Debbie read that line again, put in a joke about dirty socks, and then it was over.

"Kiss the bride!" Debbie yelled as she held up a glass of champagne.

Derek's lips met mine and all was right with the world.

"Woohoo!" Hank yelled.

I turned to find Mama and Francois both crying. We all hugged and nothing but pure joy radiated from all of us as we chatted, ate Chinese food, and drank champagne.

"We're finally married," Derek whispered in my ear as he kissed my cheek. "This is the best day of my life, Tilly."

"Same here," I murmured. "The very best day ever."

Derek, Debbie, and I returned to Oak Peak the next day. We'd set our honeymoon vacation for the summer, so for now, it was time for all of us to head home.

Carla met us at our house with our fur babies. Tinker raced toward us so fast, she actually took us both down to the ground.

"You're going to break your back if you wag that tail any harder!" I yelled as she licked my face.

Belle, on the other hand, made sure we knew how unhappy she'd been at our absence. For two days we didn't see her, then she left a hairball in my shoe. Finally, on day four after our arrival, she curled up on my lap while we all watched television.

"I'm sorry, Belly-Belle," I whispered, stroking her head. "I love you."

We settled back into our routine and I returned to work.

I'd been home a week and every day I'd kept my eye out for Deputy Byron Mills, but I had the feeling he'd been avoiding me.

As I exited the paper one afternoon, I noticed him walking down Oak Peak Avenue, so I followed him with every intention of giving him a piece of my mind for his role in my ruined wedding.

I tapped him on the shoulder and he turned around. His face paled and his eyes widened in surprise as our gazes met. If I hadn't known exactly what he'd done, I'd say I terrified him.

"T-Tilly!" he stuttered, taking a step away from me. "H-how's it going?"

"Spare me the small talk, you big, dumb jerk," I hissed. "And listen to me very carefully. I know what you did. George at Francois' Fancy Food Catering came clean and told me everything you paid him to do to ruin my wedding."

Byron's shoulders sagged and he lowered his gaze to the cement between us.

"You should be ashamed of yourself, Byron

Mills," I said, poking my finger into his chest. "Absolutely ashamed." I fought the urge to kick him in the shin. "I want to make something very, very clear to you. I love Derek. Very much. Right now, I hate you. I have never liked you enough for you to be my boyfriend, let alone my husband. I find you pretty to look at, but you bore me to tears. Do you understand? You and I are never going to be together. Never."

When our gazes met, tears welled in his eyes and I almost felt sorry for him. Almost.

"I got married, Byron," I said holding up my left hand and pointing to the wedding band. "You couldn't stop it, no matter how hard you tried."

"I'm sorry," he whispered.

"I don't care how sorry you are or how guilty you feel right now," I said. "What I want is for you to get some help. If you find it impossible to understand that there's a good chance I'll never even speak to you again, then you need therapy. Go find someone to talk to, Byron. Get on with your life because I'm getting on with mine, and you aren't part of my plans."

Turning on my heel, I flipped my hair over my shoulder and walked away. His stare bore into me, and I hoped I had made myself clear once and for all.

"I'm sorry, Tilly!" he yelled after me, but I ignored him.

My phone began to ring and I pulled it from my purse. After taking a few deep breaths, I answered it.

"Bernie!" I said, hoping I sounded as happy to speak to her as I felt. "How are you? Where are you?"

"I'm back at home," Bernie said, her voice quiet.

"What's wrong?" I asked. "Are you feeling okay?"

The last time we'd talked, she'd assured me that she'd suffered no ill-effects of being struck by lightning.

"I feel fine," she said, "but something weird is happening."

"What's that?"

"Well, I'm not sure how to put this, so I'm just going to say it and hope you don't think I'm crazy."

"Okay," I said, coming to a halt. "Tell me."

"Tilly, since I was hit by lightning, I'm seeing a ghost."

Oh, my.

***

Dear Reader:

To begin Bernie's adventure of solving crimes with her crazy, ghostly sidekick, please check out

The Guest is a Goner, book one of the Sedona Spirit series!

Looking for more of Tilly, Derek and the gang? Grab their one year update HERE!

Sedona Spirt Mysteries

As the owner of Sedona Bed and Breakfast, Bernadette Maxwell has always played up the rumors that her business was haunted. She's never believed it herself, even though she can't explain the odd odors that sometimes permeate the room or why a blast of cold air comes out of nowhere… until she has an accident and can suddenly see her resident ghost—her crazy, fun-loving, hippie grandmother, Ruby.

Killer Skies Mysteries

Set in 1965, join Patty Briggs, stewardess extraordinaire, as she flies the skies and solves murders with the help of her friends… and one cute FBI agent!

ABOUT THE AUTHOR

Carly Winter is the pen name for a USA Today best-selling and award-winning romance author.

When not writing, she likes spending time with her family, reading and enjoying the fantastic Arizona weather (except summer - she doesn't like summer). She does like dogs, wine and chocolate and wishes Christmas happened twice a year.

For more information on her books, please visit:
CarlyWinterCozyMysteries.com